Somersaults
— and —
Dreams

RISING
☆
STAR

CATE SHEARWATER

EGMONT

EGMONT

We bring stories to life

Somersaults and Dreams: Rising Star
First published in Great Britain 2015
by Egmont UK Limited
The Yellow Building, 1 Nicholas Road, London W11 4AN

Text copyright © 2015 Cate Shearwater
Illustration copyright © 2015 Jongmee

The moral rights of the author and illustrator have been asserted

ISBN 978 1 4052 6879 0

www.egmont.co.uk

A CIP catalogue record for this title is available from the British Library

56452/1

Typeset in Sabon by Avon DataSet Ltd, Bidford on Avon, Warwickshire
Printed and bound in Great Britain by CPI Group

Stay safe online. Any website addresses listed in this book are correct
at the time of going to print. However, Egmont is not responsible for
content hosted by third parties.

Please be aware that online content can be subject to change and websites can
contain content that is unsuitable for children. We advise that all children are
supervised when using the internet.

For Elsie, Nancy, Kate and Lexi –
gorgeous gym girlies!

CHAPTER
One

Ellie stood in the middle of the Olympic arena, waiting for the music to start. She shivered with fear and anticipation. This was it. Her chance to win the gold medal she'd always dreamed of. It all came down to this final routine.

The audience fell silent as the music started, a haunting strain that seemed to bring Ellie's limbs to life. It was like she was a puppet, being tugged by the strings of the melody. She forgot about the audience, forgot about the arena, forgot that she was in the biggest competition of her life as she lost herself in the magic of gymnastics.

Ellie performed as she had never performed before, leaping higher, spinning faster, tumbling more powerfully.

1

And, as the music moved towards a crescendo, she launched into her final tumble sequence. As she flew through the double pike to finish, she felt like an exotic bird, twisting a myriad of colours through the air.

And then she landed . . .

. . . and there was silence. Total silence. No applause, not a single hand clapped. Ellie glanced around breathlessly at the sea of blank faces, staring at her, unsmiling. And then, high up in the back row, someone stood up and shouted, 'This girl is not eligible to compete. She hasn't qualified for Junior British Champs!'

Ellie woke with a start. It took a second for her to register where she was: not in an Olympic arena, but on a train heading back to the London Gymnastics Academy for the start of the autumn term. She shook her head and blinked a couple of times but somehow she couldn't seem to shake off the vivid dream.

'Ah, Sleeping Beauty is awake!' said Nancy who was sitting next to her. 'Were you dreaming of gym again, Ellie?'

Ellie felt herself blushing. 'Yeah. How could you tell?'

'Oh, you were doing funny things with your hands,' said Nancy with a grin.

'*And* you were humming your floor music in your sleep!' added Tam, who was sitting across the table from Ellie.

Ellie laughed. 'No, I wasn't!'

Tam just shrugged. 'So what was it this time? Commonwealth Games . . . the World Championships . . .?'

'Olympics,' Ellie admitted.

'Ooh – I like it. Dream big!' said Nancy. 'How did you get on?'

'You realise it was only a dream – right?' Tam asked her.

'Yeah, but it could be one of those fortune-telling dreams, couldn't it!' said Nancy. 'I've had one of those. In it Sasha was telling me I was talking too much during warm-up – and then the very next day she actually did! Spooky, huh!'

'Um – that doesn't exactly take a crystal ball!' said

Tam. 'Sasha tells you off practically every other day!'

Nancy huffed loudly. 'Yeah, well, it doesn't take a fortune-teller to know that Ellie's going to make it to the Olympics either,' she declared. 'I mean, she's so dedicated she even keeps up her training in her sleep!'

Ellie laughed, and so did her two best friends. It was easy to see they were twins. Even though Tam had dark curly hair, whilst Nancy's was straight and straw-coloured, they shared the same warm chocolate-coloured eyes and upturned noses – now even more covered in freckles than ever after a fortnight in Cornwall, staying with Ellie's family.

'Anyway,' Nancy continued. 'I want to know how Ellie got on in this Olympic dream! Did you end up on the podium with a gold medal round your neck? I bet you did!'

'Sorry to disappoint you,' said Ellie with a sigh. 'But it was more of a nightmare. They kicked me out because I hadn't even qualified for Junior British Champs – let alone the Olympic team!'

'Ouch!' said Nancy, pulling a face. 'Classic anxiety

dream then. I get them all the time – only usually, in mine, I'm doing a routine in my pyjamas.'

Ellie laughed at the thought of Nancy taking to the floor at the Olympics in her fluffy, kitten-covered PJs.

'That's nothing,' said Tam. 'I once dreamed I was performing in one of Nancy's leotards!'

Nancy shrieked with laughter. 'Which one? Ooh – I bet you'd look gorgeous in my pink-and-purple comp leo – the one with all the sparkles!'

Tam rolled his eyes and Ellie glanced at him curiously. Despite being shorter than Nancy – and being born three minutes after her – Tam always seemed like the older sibling. He was calm, patient and a very talented gymnast. Ellie couldn't imagine him getting worried about anything, let alone competitions.

'I didn't think you got nervous,' she said.

Tam looked serious for a second. 'Of course I do. Everyone does.'

'But you got selected for GB Junior squad!' said Nancy. 'And you already know you're going to

British Champs. What on earth have *you* got to be worried about?'

Tam shrugged. 'I've just been really lucky this year.'

'Not lucky,' said Ellie. 'You've worked really hard. You deserve all your success – you earned it!'

'There's always an element of luck in any sport,' insisted Tam. 'I mean, if you hadn't got chickenpox last term and missed Grades you'd have qualified for Junior British Champs then. That was epic bad luck!'

'Maybe,' Ellie said, doubtfully. Privately she still wondered whether she'd have qualified, even if she hadn't been ill.

'And it's *totally* bad luck you keep shooting up like a sunflower, sis,' Tam added, helping himself to the last of the home-made Cornish pasties Ellie's mum had packed for the journey. Apart from gymnastics, there was nothing Tam loved more than food, and he seemed to be perpetually hungry.

'It's true,' said Nancy, shoving her long gangly legs out into the train corridor. 'Look at me. I'm officially the Big Friendly Giant of the Academy.'

'Which is bad luck for me because it makes me look like a hobbit,' said Tam. 'And worse luck for you because everyone knows a sudden growth spurt can throw a gymnast off her game.'

'Yeah, but it's not like that's the only reason I keep failing to qualify for British Champs,' said Nancy, pulling a face. Then she sighed. 'Maybe I'm just not good enough.'

'Of course you are!' Ellie protested. 'You are an amazing gymnast – ten times more powerful than me. I'd love to be able to vault like you do.'

'Yeah, but you know what Emma says,' said Nancy with a resigned shrug. Emma Bannerdown was the director of the London Gymnastics Academy. A former Olympian herself, she knew exactly what it took to get to the top. 'Gymnastics is not just about being physically strong. It requires mental strength too, and that means not falling to pieces in a competition.'

'Yeah, well, Emma obviously thinks you have both kinds,' said Ellie, firmly. 'Or she wouldn't be giving you another chance.'

'Or promoting you and Ellie to Pre-Elite squad,' said Tam who had polished off his pasty and was now helping himself to a tomato and chocolate muffin – one of Ellie's mum's famously bizarre recipes which usually tasted better than they looked.

'Yeah – what's all that about?' said Nancy. 'When neither of us have qualified for the Junior British.'

'Emma must think that you and Ellie will qualify via the Challenge Cup,' said Tam. 'Which is definitely not easy, so she must really believe in you! That's why she promoted you early.'

Ellie's stomach did a flip at the mention of the Challenge Cup, the make-or-break competition that took place just before Christmas. It was her last chance to qualify for Junior British Champs next term and become an elite gymnast. 'It seems like such a long shot.'

'Well, I don't care why she promoted us,' Nancy was saying. 'We're going to feel so grown up compared to the babies in Development Squad. *And* we're going to be training with Oleg!'

'That's definitely NOT going to be easy!' said

Tam and they all laughed. Oleg Petrescu was the kindly but eccentric gymnastic coach of the Pre-Elite squad. He was Romanian and he was famous for his rather unusual training methods.

'Did you hear he spent the summer in Romania?' said Tam. 'He's come back determined to be much stricter – the way they are over there. So you'd better watch out, girls!'

'Ellie and I can cope with Oleg, can't we?' said Nancy with a giant grin. 'Anyway, I reckon my muscles are twice the size they used to be after all the rowing I've done in the past two weeks!'

She bared her arms, which were indeed looking incredibly toned – even for a gymnast. The three of them, plus Ellie's little sister Lucy, had spent nearly every day of their holiday out on the water, rowing, crabbing, sailing and messing about on Trengilly Creek. Nancy was a natural and could beat the others easily in a rowing race – even Ellie, who'd been rowing all her life.

'Hey, and did you hear that Toni Nimakov found some gymnastic prodigy in a circus?' Tam went on, searching around in the cool bag for more food. 'He's brought her back to the Academy!'

Toni Nimakov was a four-time Olympic gold medallist who had coached the very best gymnasts in the world and trained the Elite squad at the Academy. He was terrifyingly strict but brilliant.

'How do you know all this stuff?' Nancy demanded.

'I have my sources,' grinned Tam, pulling out three little bags of fudge Lucy had made for them as leaving presents. Each was tied with a different coloured ribbon and had a hand-drawn label with their name on it. Looking at the effort that Lucy had put into them made Ellie feel a pang of sadness. She wished she didn't have to leave her little sister behind each term.

'Don't make out like you're some kind of super-spy,' Nancy was saying as Tam tossed over her bag of fudge and started munching on his own. 'You've probably just been on Facebook with Robbie Sipson. He's the worst gossip ever.' Robbie was one of the other boys at the Academy. He and Tam had become more friendly this summer, although Nancy thought he was irritating and even Ellie couldn't figure out what Tam saw in him.

'Never mind how he found out,' said Ellie. 'Did this girl really come from the circus? Doesn't she have any formal gym training at all?'

'Apparently not,' said Tam.

Ellie was surprised. She remembered how hard it had been for her to start at the Academy behind the others last year. If the new girl had never been trained at all, it would be even harder for her. 'How old is she?' she asked. 'What squad is she going into?'

'Robbie said she's twelve, so I guess she'll be going into Development Squad, one below you guys,' said Tam. 'She's meant to be incredible on floor and beam, but she's never done the bars in her life!'

'Ooh, I can't wait to see this!' said Nancy. 'A girl who's been swinging on the trapeze and walking the tightrope making a splash at the Academy! Scarlett is going to be up in arms about it.'

Ellie sighed at the mention of Scarlett Atkins.

Scarlett resented anyone she thought showed talent and might be a threat to her Queen of the Beam status (or Queen of Mean, if you asked Nancy). She had made life really difficult for Ellie last year. Luckily Nancy and the other girls had made her feel welcome – Ellie made a silent promise to herself to do the same for the younger circus girl.

Ellie turned and glanced out of the window. The train was on the outskirts of London now and the green fields had been replaced by rows of terraces. She felt a flutter of excitement as they neared the city. The summer had been magical and it was so tough saying goodbye to her family – especially Lucy – but it was brilliant to be back in London, about to start a new year at the Academy.

'I'm missing the beach already!' said Nancy glumly, staring at the London houses. 'I mean, I can't wait to see Mum and all the girls, but remind me again why we want to spend twenty-five hours a week in a stuffy gym being tortured by slave-driver coaches?'

'Twenty-seven and a half hours,' Tam reminded

her. 'Pre-Elite squad train for longer!'

'What joy!' said Nancy, pulling a face.

'Isn't it!' asked Ellie, who would happily spend every hour of every day in the gym.

'Um – I was being sarcastic,' said Nancy.

'I know you were,' said Ellie. 'But this is going to be the best term ever. Just you wait and see.'

CHAPTER
Two

It was great to be back at Head-Over-Heels House, the large, tumbledown building that was home to all of the out-of-towners, the Academy students who boarded during term time. Ellie and the twins were dying to see all their old friends, but when they walked through the front door they found the house practically deserted.

'What's going on, Mum?' asked Nancy, giving her mother Mandy Moffat a massive hug before flinging her luggage down in the hallway. 'Where is everyone?'

Mandy wasn't just the twins' mum; she was also

Head-Over-Heels housemother, which meant she looked after all the gymnasts who boarded there. She made sure they were fed and clothed, and she also helped them through all the ups and downs of gymnastic life. Ellie wasn't sure what they'd do without her.

'You'd better go out to the garden and take a look at what's going on!' said Mandy with a smile. 'I must admit, I've never seen anything like it.'

'Sounds exciting!' said Tam, giving his mum a quick peck on the cheek before dumping his stuff on top of Nancy's and heading for the patio doors. 'Cheers, Mum! Come on, girls. Let's check it out.'

'Oh, how I've missed clearing up after you two!' laughed Mandy as the twins sped outside, leaving bags scattered everywhere. Ellie followed them.

They made their way out into the back garden to find lots of the other Academy students scattered over the grass on an assortment of rugs and deckchairs. There was copper-headed Robbie from the boys' squad, and Kashvi, Camille and Bella from the girls'. Even Sian Edwards – the most Senior gymnast at the Academy who'd won a medal at the last Olympics – was there. And there was Scarlett, lying in a sun-lounger wearing a giant pair of shades and a scowl and glaring hard at something on the other side of the garden. They looked to see what had caught her attention. 'What on earth . . . oh!' said Nancy.

A washing line was strung across the garden. It ran from the low kitchen roof over to the red brick wall at the end of the garden, fixed carefully at each end. And walking along it – as if it were the most natural thing to do in the world – was a girl that Ellie had never seen before. A tiny pixie-like creature with white blonde flyaway hair and a face that twinkled like a cheeky little elf. And she was gliding like an ice skater along the thin strip of rope without the teeniest hint of a wobble.

'Whoa!' breathed Tam.

'How is that even possible?' said Ellie. 'It's just a flimsy bit of rope!'

'She must be some kind of fairy,' said Nancy. 'With invisible wings or magic space dust or something!'

'Amazing, isn't it?' said Bella, a tiny dark-haired girl with a wise face and two little buns which looked like monkey ears.

'Yeah, an' she's been up there all morning,' said Robbie. 'Walking along the fence post too – and the ridge pole of the kitchen roof. She's a nutter if you ask me!'

'Seriously?' said Tam, looking at the younger girl in admiration. 'And Mum let her?'

'She made her get off the roof,' said Scarlett loudly from her sun-lounger. 'And she did tell her not to walk the washing line either, but Katya seems determined to ignore instructions.'

'Katya?' said Ellie.

'Katya Popolova,' said Kashvi, an Indian girl as pretty as a princess who dressed like a tomboy and talked like a cockney street urchin. 'She's Russian.'

'Ah – so she's the girl Toni found?' said Tam. 'Well, I can see what he saw in her. She's amazing.'

'Talented but totally undisciplined,' sniffed Scarlett.

Ellie glanced at Scarlett, who was looking as glamorous and groomed as always. She should have

17

been beautiful with her creamy complexion, sheet of long blonde hair and startling green eyes, but there was something about the permanently dissatisfied expression that she wore, and the condescending spark in her eyes, that spoilt her otherwise perfect looks.

'She'll never make a gymnast,' Scarlett went on. 'She's all showy moves with no polish.'

'Then the Academy will give her polish,' said Nancy.

'Really? It never worked for you, Nancy Moffat,' said Scarlett with a silky smile.

Robbie sniggered and Tam glared at him.

'*You* need to polish up your people skills, Scarlett,' said Tam. He might spend most of the time teasing Nancy, but there was no way he was letting anyone else do it.

'I'm just saying that Katya Popup, or whatever her name is, won't last five minutes at the Academy,' said Scarlett with a shrug. 'Gymnastics is about discipline, precision, focus – not about silly circus tricks and showing off.'

'Camille – wow – I love your new hair,' said Nancy, rolling her eyes and deliberately changing the subject. 'Did you get it done in Paris?'

Camille Bertinet was sporting a very stylish new hairstyle – cut in a gamine bob that would have looked boyish on somebody else but which seemed chic and super cool on the young French gymnast.

'Oui – no more buns for me!' she said with a very elegant French shrug.

'Lucky you!' said Nancy. 'Mum scrapes my hair back so tight for competitions, I feel like I've had a facelift.'

'I swear you've grown again, Nancy!' said Kashvi

'Don't remind me!' said Nancy. 'I've been drinking gallons of dandelion tea because I read somewhere that it stunts your growth, but it's not working! I keep shooting up like a beanpole.'

Ellie grinned happily. She was thrilled to be reunited with her squad mates who she hadn't seen all summer. Even Sian Edwards had greeted Ellie with a big hug. 'You look brown as a nut,' she laughed. 'Did you spend the whole summer practicing gymnastics on that beach of yours?'

'Yes, but we did loads of other things too,' said Ellie. 'Surfing and kayaking. Nancy even wanted to go cliff-jumping, but we figured Emma would kill us if we brought her back with a broken arm!'

'Glad to hear you had some fun,' said Sian, grinning at Ellie like a protective older sister. 'And came back in one piece!'

Scarlett was still scowling.

'Scarlett, don't you know if the wind changes your face will get stuck in that sour expression forever?' asked Nancy.

Just at that moment, Katya Popolova descended from the washing line in a double somersault, landing on the grass just centimetres from where the girls were standing. She finished with a funny little flourish, two bright violet eyes sparkling at everyone and a smile spreading from ear to ear.

She looked even tinier on the grass – especially next to Nancy. If they hadn't been told she was twelve years old, Ellie would have taken her for not much more than eight or nine.

'I am Katya Popolova,' the small girl piped up. 'What are your names?'

'I am Nancy Moffat,' said Nancy, grinning and extending a polite hand to the smaller girl. 'This is Ellie Trengilly.'

Katya's face lit up. 'Oh, I am so pleased to meet you!' she said, launching herself at Nancy, wrapping her arms around her waist and hugging her tightly, before turning and doing the same to Ellie, much to both girls' surprise. 'Your mother say we will share a room,' said Katya, smiling from Ellie to Nancy happily.

'Well, that's cool,' Nancy grinned. 'It'll be a bit of a squish but the more the merrier – right, Ellie?'

'Totally,' said Ellie who had taken an instant liking to the tiny tightrope-walking circus girl.

'And this – he must be Tam – your brother?' said Katya, grabbing Tam and giving him a kiss on both cheeks that made him go bright red. 'You have the same eyes.'

'Um – yes!' Tam blurted, stepping back nervously

as Robbie practically collapsed with laughter.

'What you were doing on the washing line was amazing!' said Ellie. The beam had always been Ellie's toughest piece of apparatus, so to see how Katya managed to perform so effortlessly on an even narrower surface was amazing. Ellie wondered what her secret was. 'How do you do it?'

'Oh, I learnt to walk on high wire when I was small,' said Katya. Her face lit up like a sparkler again. 'You want me to show you now? Is easy!'

Ellie hesitated. It was incredibly tempting, but she was pretty sure Emma Bannerdown would go mad if she saw any of her gymnasts risking their bodies like that. A gymnast's career could be destroyed by injury. Ellie was aware of this better than anyone: her own Aunt Lizzie's Olympic gymnastics dream had ended that way.

So, no matter how tempting it was, Ellie figured she should play it safe. Luckily she didn't have to disappoint Katya, because just then Mandy called all the gymnasts in for supper.

'Oh good! My tummy is bumbling!' said Katya.

'Do you mean rumbling?' asked Nancy.

'Exactly,' said Katya, linking arms with Nancy and Ellie and dragging them into the house. 'Let's eat!'

CHAPTER
Three

'So tell us again what happened, Katya?' Sian Edwards was saying, as the gymnasts sat around the giant kitchen table in the basement of Head-Over-Heels House, tucking into a supper of salad and cold roast chicken. Sian and Sophia, another of the Senior Elite girls, shared a flat at the top of the house, but they always took an interest in the younger girls. And it was impossible not to be interested in Katya Popolova.

'My family runs Popolov Circus in Moscow,' said Katya, who was already on her third helping. 'Three generations all work together.'

'And does everyone perform in the show?' asked Kashvi, who was sitting astride a chair and staring at Katya in wide-eyed amazement.

'Yes! My grandfather, he is clown,' Katya explained. 'My father does trapeze and high wire. My little brother Pietr is world's smallest strongman, and my grandmother does acrobatics on horseback . . .'

'Your grandma?' asked Ellie with a look of surprise.

'Oh, yes,' said Katya, like it was no big deal to have a somersaulting granny.

'And you?' asked Tam. He had just about recovered from Katya's kiss attack, but he had sat down on the opposite side of the table just to be on the safe side. 'What can you do?'

'I do many things,' said Katya, helping herself to another baked potato. 'Juggling, trapeze, high wire, tumbling, unicycle . . .'

'Wow! Who trained you?' asked Nancy.

'Oh, circus is like one big family – everyone helps.' For a second Katya's twinkling eyes clouded a little and Ellie realised how hard it must be for her, knowing her family were thousands of miles away.

'OK, so tell us what happened with Toni,' said Tam.

Ellie saw some of the others leaning forward, intrigued to know exactly how a small circus girl from Russia had ended up at one of the most prestigious gymnastic academies in Britain.

'Is all big surprise!' said Katya. 'Toni, he come home to Russia to see his family – he is also Russian, you know. He comes to circus one night . . .'

'. . . and sees you,' added Bella.

'And the next minute he's whizzing you back to England!' Robbie concluded. 'Blimey – that's all a bit like something out of a movie!'

'It's all a bit odd, if you ask me!' said Scarlett. 'I mean, it sounds too much like a coincidence – unless you're going to tell us your uncle was an ex-international gymnast or something.'

She look pointedly at Ellie as she said this and Ellie knew what she was thinking – Scarlett never missed an opportunity to make Ellie feel like she had only won her scholarship to the Academy because of her Aunt Lizzie's success.

'No, all my family are circus people,' said Katya. 'Is just my lucky stars that Toni comes that night!'

'What did I tell you about luck!' said Tam, grinning at Ellie and Nancy.

'You must miss your parents,' said Bella.

'My mother died when Pietr was born,' Katya said, quietly. 'And my father think it is good for me to go to English school, and to have proper gymnastics training in one of the best academies in the world.' She smiled again. 'There he is right! But, yes, I do miss them – my brother Pietr especially.'

'And the animals,' said Robbie cheekily. 'You must miss them.'

'Yes, even them,' Katya laughed. 'I want to bring my favourite dog to Head-Over-Heels House but they say this is not possible.'

'I've been trying to persuade Mum that we should get a Head-Over-Heels puppy for years,' said Tam.

'Maybe Katya could train it up and take it to Junior British Champs!' said Nancy.

'Well, obviously, Katya won't be going to

Champs,' said Scarlett snootily.

'Um – why not?' asked Nancy.

'Duh! Because she's not actually British!'

'My mother she from England,' said Katya. 'So Toni say I am allowed to compete over here too.'

'Oh,' said Scarlett, unable to hide her disappointment. 'Well, only gymnasts who've qualified are eligible,' she added. 'Or perhaps you've failed so often you've forgotten that, Nancy?'

'Then she'll just have to qualify at the Challenge Cup!' said Nancy through gritted teeth. 'Just like me and Ellie.'

Ellie's heart did a somersault. For a few moments she'd forgotten her fears about the make-or-break competition but now they all came flooding back.

'There's no way she'll be ready for a major competition this term,' said Scarlett. I doubt she even knows the rules!'

'In circus there are no rules!' Katya declared happily. 'Is all about entertainment.'

'Blimey!' said Kashvi. 'You're going to get the shock of your life at the Academy then.'

'Oui – gymnastics ees all about ze rules,' added Camille.

'And if you go breaking them you'll be out of the Academy before you can say big top!' said Scarlett smugly.

It was quite a squash in the room the girls were sharing. Mandy had moved in the old bunk bed that Tam and Nancy had used as kids and squeezed in another small chest of drawers. Nancy didn't mind sharing with Katya, although she insisted on getting the top bunk.

'Tam made me sleep on the bottom for years,' she said. 'Even though I was way too tall and forever bashing my head – I was black and blue all the time!'

Katya was thrilled with the bottom bunk. In fact, Katya was thrilled with everything. She seemed to have a permanent smile on her face, and she hugged and kissed anyone who came within a five metre radius of her – probably why Tam had offered to wash up rather than help the girls unpack.

'I sleep always in different places,' Katya told Ellie

and Nancy, as she clambered happily into bed that night. 'In circus you move around a lot. Different town every month.'

'So how did you go to school?' asked Nancy.

'Oh, no school,' said Katya. 'My grandmother teach me.'

'No school!' said Nancy. 'How cool is that! We do reduced school hours to fit in with our training, but we still have to keep up with our work. The Academy is really strict about that.'

'But it's fun,' said Ellie, to reassure Katya. 'School's nice and the Academy is amazing. Just you wait – you're going to love it!'

'And you can forget about what Scarlett said,' Nancy added. 'Cos you're going to totally rock it as an Academy girl!'

Ellie lay awake for a while after the others had dropped off. She always found it strange when she first came back to London, getting used to the night-time sounds of the city, so different to the soft lapping of the waves on Trengilly beach that she could hear from her bedroom at home. But it wasn't just that stopping Ellie from sleeping. She couldn't stop thinking about the dream she'd had on the train, and about the Challenge Cup – what would happen if she didn't qualify this time round?

She *had* to qualify. Because if she didn't, she'd lose her scholarship. Ellie's parents were already making huge sacrifices to send her to the Academy, and there was no way they'd be able to manage it without the scholarship money. So, there was a lot more than just Ellie's pride riding on the Challenge Cup – her whole future at the Academy depended on it. Even with the two other girls sleeping next to her in the room, Ellie suddenly felt very lonely.

CHAPTER
Four

In the early-morning September sunshine, the red brick building of the Academy shone brightly as a gaggle of Academy students sat on the steps, catching up on summer gossip before training began. As she approached, Ellie felt the same thrill of excitement she'd experienced on her very first day, last year. She reckoned she'd always feel that same buzz, however long she kept going.

Katya bounced up the steps beside her and Ellie grinned.

'It's like having a puppy,' Tam joked, waving good-bye to the girls as he headed off into the boys' gym.

Ellie and Nancy showed Katya to the girls' changing room, where they found a gaggle of smaller gymnasts giggling in a corner. The younger girls fell silent at the sight of the two Pre-Elite girls.

'Ah – the new kids in Development,' said Nancy. 'They make me feel so old and wise!'

'You might be old but you'll never be wise, Nancy!' said Ellie with a grin. She recognised several of the younger girls who had been in Beginner's squad last term, and she introduced them to Katya as the people she would be training with. Katya greeted every single one of them with a giant bear hug.

'She doesn't seem to have any problem making friends, does she?' Nancy observed as she and Ellie pulled off their tracksuits and tugged their hair into ponytails, ready for training.

Katya was already giggling and swapping scrunchies with a girl who had a doll-like face and curly brown hair that fell in ringlets nearly as far as her bottom.

'Who's that?' asked Ellie.

'I haven't seen her before,' said Nancy. 'I guess she must be new too.'

They didn't have to wait long to find out the identity of Katya's new friend. As the other members of Development headed off for warm-up, Katya tugged the little girl over to Ellie and Nancy.

'Nancy, Ellie – this my new friend Lexi Davies!' she squeaked.

'Hello,' said Lexi, blushing a deep crimson and lowering her eyes.

'Lexi is new to Academy – like me,' Katya declared.

'We didn't think we'd seen you before,' said Ellie. 'Where have you come from?'

'I was training in Liverpool,' Lexi explained shyly. 'But my father got a new job, so we had to move.'

'Oh, Liverpool is a great gym,' said Ellie.

'Even if they are our biggest rivals,' added Nancy with a grin. 'Were you training with Eva Reddle?'

'Oh yes!' Lexi's eyes lit up. 'She's absolutely lovely – and she's the Junior British Champion, you know.'

'She is for now,' said Scarlett, who had just appeared in the changing room, sporting a new leotard and matching training shorts with her name emblazoned in diamantés across her bottom. 'Until I knock her off the top spot, that is!'

'Oh, so you reckon you're going to win gold at British Champs now?' asked Nancy, rolling her eyes.

'Just watch me!' said Scarlett coolly, picking up her guard bag which she'd forgotten. 'Oh no, you won't be able to – because you haven't even qualified yet!'

'Well I only started at the Academy in January,' Ellie told Lexi, changing the subject quickly. 'But everyone was really nice . . .'

'Nearly everyone!' said Nancy, rolling her eyes in Scarlett's direction.

'And your coach, Sasha, she's super lovely!' said Ellie, who kind of wished she was still training with her old coach who'd helped her so much.

'Unless you get on the wrong side of her,' added Scarlett, pulling a diamanté-studded scrunchie over her perfect bun. 'If you do that she's super strict, the scariest coach in the whole gym.'

'I am not scared of Sasha Darling,' said Katya with a little shrug. 'I hear she was once in circus like me, so I think we will get on very well. Just like friends!'

'Well, you're not going to get on well if you're late!' said Nancy. 'Come on!'

The girls all hurried into the gym. Ellie and Nancy waved goodbye to Katya and Lexi and went to join the other Pre-Elite girls, who were already lined up on the blue mat waiting for Oleg Petrescu.

The eccentric and brilliant coach had once been an international gymnast, training alongside many of the greats. He had a reputation for being fierce one minute and cuddly the next. 'A bit like a bear,' Nancy whispered as they waited for him to come over. 'Only you don't know if he's going to be a teddy bear or a grizzly from one minute to the next.'

Oleg had a comical appearance. Like many gymnasts he was small, but since he had retired from competing he was nearly as round as he was tall. He had a large curling moustache like an old-fashioned strongman, and he liked to wear flamboyantly coloured tracksuits, usually in patterns that were about twenty years out of date.

Today he was looking incredibly fierce, despite sporting a pink and yellow tracksuit in a shiny material that made him look a bit like a small round spaceman. He did not even smile as he walked along the line of gymnasts, inspecting each of them as if he were a sergeant-major in front of a parade. Ellie felt nerves flutter in her stomach.

'This year I am bringing a new regime to the Academy,' Oleg announced in a loud booming voice that seemed too big for his little body. 'In holidays I spend time in Romanian gymnastic school, where I train as boy. Things are very different over there.'

'Uh-oh,' whispered Nancy under her breath. 'This sounds worrying.'

Oleg shot her a look. 'In Romania, coach is like god,' he said, his voice booming off the high roof of the gym. 'The gymnasts, they obey without question.'

'He thinks he's a god now?' whispered Kashvi.

'In England there is not so good discipline,' said Oleg glaring even more fiercely. 'But in Oleg's class, no more!' he declared, waving his arms wildly to stress his point. Next to her, Ellie could feel Nancy trying hard not to giggle. 'We will train Romanian-style. We will work like in army – bootcamp, drill, silence! And in this way I will make great gymnasts of you all.'

Bootcamp – army style – drills! This was worse than Oleg's healthy eating obsession! Ellie glanced at Camille, Kashvi and Bella, all of whom were looking as alarmed as she felt. Of course, Scarlett wore her usual smug smile, as if she had nothing to fear from Oleg's terrifying new training regime.

'Well, I might as well give up now,' muttered Nancy.

'Does anyone want to quit?' asked Oleg, fixing his stare on Nancy, his eyes bulging. 'Because if you cannot take the heat, is time to get out of Oleg's kitchen.'

'Um . . .' Nancy started to say, but Ellie jabbed her hard in the ribs.

'You!' said Oleg, transferring his gaze to Ellie and eyeballing her suspiciously. 'You are Elizabeth Trengilly, right?'

'Um – yes,' said Ellie, colouring as Nancy let out a snigger next to her. No one ever called her Elizabeth, and very few people even knew she'd been named after her Aunt Lizzie.

'So you and this giggling girl here,' Oleg glared fiercely at Nancy, who instantly stopped sniggering, 'you must do Challenge Cup if you are to qualify for British Champs.'

'Yes,' said Ellie. Nancy nodded seriously.

'I ask myself if you are even ready for Pre-Elite, but Emma say you will prove yourselves. I hope this is right.'

Ellie's stomach did a flip. 'We'll try,' she said.

'Try is not good enough for Oleg!' he barked. 'You must succeed – or is back to Miss Darling and her babies for you both, understood?'

Ellie nodded. She glanced over to where Sasha Darling was talking to the scared-looking bunch of new Development kids. She might miss her old coach, but there was no way she wanted to be demoted, and she silently vowed to work so hard that Oleg would never even think of it again.

'Good, then let us begin!'

CHAPTER
Five

The Pre-Elite girls quickly got an idea of exactly what Sergeant Oleg's training regime involved. First he put them through the most gruelling warm-up they'd ever done in their lives. 'No amount of medals could ever be worth this pain!' Nancy observed as Oleg made them hold the plank position for a whole five minutes before making them do two hundred sit-ups in a row.

Then he presented each of them with a training schedule, broken up into ten minute segments of intense repetitions to be completed at top speed. At the end of each segment, Oleg blew a whistle.

'He thinks he ees ze football ref now!' whispered Camille as the girls passed between rotations.

'SILENCE!' Oleg's voice boomed out, echoing off the high ceiling of the gym. 'No slacking, no chatting, no daydreaming – just work, work, work until you drop.'

But in fact the silence rule wasn't necessary, because if they were going to complete each of the ten-minute rotations they barely had to breathe, let along gossip.

It was pretty intense. In the floor segment, Ellie had to complete three back to back versions of her floor routine, followed by a series of tumbles onto a pile of mats. Then on to the bar, where she had to do sets of top turns, upstart handstands and giants. And the same again on the beam and vault, plus conditioning circuits in between.

As they went along, Oleg stood watching, frowning and occasionally calling out things like, 'Pull your arm back quicker on the dismount,' or, 'You're not finishing into corners'. It was completely unlike the way they'd trained under Sasha, but to her surprise

Ellie found that she really took to it. The new intensity was exhilarating, and she liked the way they were each responsible for their own training programme. They could choose to slack and not complete their repetitions in the set time – or they could rise to the challenge. Ellie had always been self-disciplined, so Oleg's style suited her perfectly. And there was no time to think of anything but gymnastics, which was kind of wonderful!

On the beam Ellie even managed to perfect flipping over in her tricky front salto followed by a sheep jump. They were both moves she'd done before but the really difficult bit was connecting the two together. Each time she had tried it in the past she had lost forwards momentum and started to wobble.

But then Ellie recalled Katya on the washing line – the way she'd seemed to glide rather than walk, how she'd barely seemed to need the rope to support her at all. Ellie decided to pretend she was on the high wire with just a flimsy piece of string beneath her feet, the only thing keeping her upright the sharp stillness of her body. She tried the move again, flipping up, back and around, and then as she came into the connection she pulled herself sharply upwards, defying the downwards pull of gravity. She imagined that she wasn't aiming to land on a strip of wood ten centimetres wide, but a tiny sliver of rope.

And it worked. She moved effortlessly from move to move and landed without a wobble. As she came back down to earth she heard a voice from behind her say, 'Better.'

Ellie nearly fell off when she realised Oleg was talking to her. She'd been so engrossed in practising that she hadn't even noticed the coach come over to watch her.

'Thank you,' she managed to stammer. 'I think maybe I could try a layout with the sheep jump too.'

But Oleg shook his head. 'Now is not time for learning new moves,' he said firmly. 'You want to qualify at the Challenge Cup, you cannot afford to make mistakes. You play it safe. Stick with what you know.'

'But if I could put in some new skills, raise my difficulty levels . . .'

'Forget about difficulty,' said Oleg. 'When you prepare for competition, you must think only execution! Execution! Execution!'

Then he moved away. Ellie's heart sank, particularly when she saw Camille working on a new vault and Bella practising a new skill on the bar, but she knew Oleg was right. For now, she just needed to focus on qualifying. Ellie gritted her teeth and pulled herself back up on to the beam.

Not everyone was so sure about Oleg's new approach, though. In the changing room after the first session, Nancy declared, 'I'm a gymnast – get me out of here!'

'It wasn't *that* bad,' said Bella, who was pulling on her school uniform.

'It's the silence that gets me,' said Kashvi, tying her school tie in a messy knot.

'Oui! I 'ave never seen Nancy keep quiet for

so long in all 'er life,' remarked Camille, and the others all giggled.

'Well, I rather enjoyed a rest from the incessant chatter,' said Scarlett who was brushing out her golden hair in long even strokes. 'And I found Oleg's style of training refreshing. But perhaps it requires a dedication and focus that some of *you* don't have.'

She looked pointedly at Nancy as she said this. Nancy was about to say something cutting in response, but at that moment Katya appeared along with the rest of Development squad. She was looking very glum.

'What's the matter?' Ellie asked.

'I do not like that Sasha Darling!' declared Katya. 'She make me do cartwheels and round-offs all morning.'

'*Just* cartwheels and round-offs?' asked Ellie, confused. It didn't sound like the inspirational coach she remembered from Development squad.

'And walking,' said Katya, her big violet eyes flashing crossly.

'Walking?' said Nancy.

'She said Katya doesn't walk right,' explained Lexi. 'Because she's so bendy from the circus.'

Katya wiggled like a worm as if to demonstrate. 'She tell me I learn bad habits and I have to unlearn them.'

'Oh, she did that to me last year,' said Nancy with a shrug. 'Don't stress about it!'

'She's right. Sometimes Sasha makes you go right back to basics to unpick bad habits you've got into,' Ellie explained.

Katya sighed theatrically and slumped down on to the bench.

'Did something else happen?' asked Nancy.

Katya shrugged. 'Well, at the end of session I get a little bit bored,' she said.

'Yes?' asked Nancy curiously. 'And . . .?'

'And I am deciding to show the girls my Chinese pole routine on the ropes.'

'What?' gasped Kashvi.

'Without Sasha's permission?' said Bella.

'And she caught you?' asked Nancy, who knew

better than anyone what Sasha could be like when she got mad.

Katya nodded, half apologetically, half gleefully. 'In middle of the chopper.'

'Um – what's the chopper?' asked Ellie curiously.

'She climbed up the rope like a monkey,' explained Lexi, eyes bright with admiration. 'Then when she was at the very top she sort of turned upside down, in the splits and spun around. It was incredible! Even the way she climbed the rope – like she was walking up it horizontally.'

'I learn to do that when I was three year old,' said Katya, without a hint of bragging in her voice.

'I wish we'd seen it!' said Nancy. 'It must have been while Oleg was making us do that horrible warm-down in the studio.'

'So zen what happened?' asked Camille.

'Did she fall?' asked Bella her face creased in concern.

'No, but – um – then Sasha turned around,' said Lexi.

'Uh-oh – you unleashed the pink fury!' said Nancy.

'She shout at me to come down right away,' said Katya, pulling on her school skirt back to front. 'Then she talk very, very fast about not being in circus now . . . '

'Then she made her do more walking,' said Lexi sympathetically.

'Walking and walking,' said Katya, dolefully buttoning up her school blouse. 'It's not very much fun!'

'So you haven't exactly had the best first session!' said Ellie, smiling sympathetically.

'Well, it will get a lot worse if you're late for school too,' said Nancy, glancing at her watch. 'Which we are all going to be if we don't get a wiggle on.'

Katya grinned. 'Ooh, I am good at that!' she said, and she wiggled enthusiastically.

CHAPTER
Six

When Ellie Skyped home that night, she already had so much news to fill her sister in on.

'Are you learning loads of cool new stuff?' asked Lucy, who wanted to know every single thing about her first day back.

'Not exactly,' said Ellie, feeling a twinge of anxiety in her stomach again. 'Oleg wants me to focus on perfecting my routines with the competition coming up.'

'Ooh, Fran says the same,' said Lucy. Fran was Ellie's old coach from her Cornish gym, the place Lucy still trained. 'She says if you rush into new moves before you're ready you risk injuries.'

'I know . . .' said Ellie, without much enthusiasm. 'So hey, how's your gym coming on?'

'I've got my Grade Four coming up,' said Lucy, excitedly. 'I'm determined to ace it, cos if I do then Fran says maybe I can try out for the Academy next year.'

'Wow,' said Ellie. 'It would be so amazing if you were here too!' She really missed her sister. There was no one at the Academy who understood what it was like to be Lizzie Trengilly's niece at the Academy like Lucy!

'Dad keeps saying he'll need to win the lottery if he has two daughters at the Academy,' giggled Lucy. Then she frowned. 'But if I got a scholarship like you, we could make it work, couldn't we?'

'Of course we could,' said Ellie, sounding more confident than she felt. The truth was that Mum and Dad could barely afford to keep Ellie at the Academy even with the scholarship. How would they cope with two daughters? But she pushed these thoughts to one side so they didn't show on her

51

face. 'You just concentrate on gym and forget about all the rest.'

But Ellie couldn't push her nagging anxiety out of her mind. She was still thinking about it when she and Nancy bumped into Emma Bannerdown as they were making their way into the changing rooms the next day.

'Ah, Ellie, Nancy, nice to see you,' Emma said. She looked both girls up and down with her cool, appraising grey eyes. 'Did you have a nice summer break?'

'The best!' said Nancy. 'We spent two whole weeks in Cornwall messing about in boats – it was epic!'

Ellie just nodded. She still felt shy in front of the Academy's director and head coach. Emma had not only been an Olympic great but also a training partner of her Aunt Lizzie.

'Well, this is a big term for both of you,' Emma said. 'Junior British Champs are only a couple of months after the Challenge Cup, so you two won't have much time after you've qualified.'

'*If* we qualify,' muttered Nancy.

Emma looked at her closely. With her cropped blonde hair, angular figure and stern features, she could appear strict and aloof, but Ellie knew that she cared a great deal about all her gymnasts. 'Well, if you go in with that attitude, you've failed before you start,' she said after a pause. 'You do *want* to qualify, right?'

'Of course,' said Nancy quietly.

Ellie risked a glance at her friend. She didn't sound very confident.

'I have no doubt in my mind that both of you are capable of qualifying,' said Emma. 'You both have more than enough talent – it's just bad luck that you haven't qualified already.'

Ellie's heart leapt and Nancy shrugged but did not look convinced.

'And the only thing that can stop you now is yourselves,' Emma went on. 'Nancy, you've lost your nerve so you need to find it again – and fast. And as for you, Ellie . . .'

'I think I need to work on some new skills for my

53

routines,' Ellie blurted out without thinking.

Emma looked at her curiously. 'What makes you say that?'

'Oleg wants me to play it safe,' she said, unable to stop now she'd started. 'But if I have higher difficulty values I can get better scores.'

'You are also more likely to make mistakes, which will cost you execution marks,' said Emma. 'I'm afraid I agree with Coach Petrescu. The lead-up to a competition is not the time to work on new skills.'

'But why did you move us to Pre-Elite if you didn't want us to work on new stuff?' asked Nancy, voicing exactly what Ellie had been thinking.

Emma smiled, as if she was pleased to see a spark of the old ambition back in Nancy's eye. 'What you need to remember is that Coach Petrescu trained and competed under the old scoring system,' she explained. 'Back in the days of the perfect ten.'

'But things have totally changed since then,' said Nancy.

'And perfect tens don't even exist any more,' Ellie added.

'Ah, but in Oleg's mind, they still do,' smiled Emma. 'And he's right in a way. No matter what difficulty score your routine is awarded, every gymnast should aim to keep her perfect ten execution points all the way through the routine. No deductions. And Oleg is the best coach to help you get competition-ready. He will make you practice, practice, practice until you are perfect!'

Ellie sighed. She loved the idea of aiming for the perfect ten every time, but it sounded like an impossible ideal to live up to.

'Don't look so worried,' said Emma, breaking into one of her rare smiles. 'I do have something new for you both to work on this term, but it's a surprise.'

'Ooh – what?' asked Nancy, who loved surprises.

'You'll have to wait and see,' said Emma, firmly. 'But for now, get back to bootcamp – or Sergeant Oleg will be on the warpath!'

'Perfect tens! No deductions!' wailed Nancy, as the girls made their way into the changing rooms. 'How is that even possible?'

'I don't think it is,' said Ellie quietly.

'You know me. I do power, not perfection,' said Nancy. 'And you're all about the artistry – that's what marks you out as a gymnast.'

'I suppose we need all three,' said Ellie, pulling off her tracksuit. 'Power, precision *and* performance. That's how the scoring system works, after all.'

'Yeah, well, the new gymnastics scoring system has got to be the most complicated in the world!' Nancy said, flinging her tracksuit in a messy heap on the floor. 'Difficulty tariffs, compulsory elements, marks for linking moves together, points for artistry, *blah, blah, blah!* With rowing it's simple – row faster! End of!'

Ellie sighed. She wasn't sure it made any more sense to her than it did to Nancy.

'Oh, take me back to the seaside and stick me in a rowing boat!' said Nancy, tossing her hand-guard bag over her shoulder and heading into the gym. 'This is all too much for me.'

CHAPTER
Seven

After her conversation with Emma, Ellie resolved to stop stressing about learning new moves and throw everything into Oleg's training regime. Emma was right – repetition was perfect for polishing her skills. And even though Nancy complained that all Oleg did was wander around barking things at them, his little comments were actually so spot on that Ellie found she was making tiny improvements on every piece of apparatus.

'But he expects us to get everything right every single time,' Nancy complained. 'That's, like, impossible!'

Unluckily for Nancy, Oleg didn't seem to have the word 'impossible' in his vocabulary. Instead, his mantra was: 'Try, try and try again.' And if you still didn't do it quite how he wanted it: 'Go back and try harder.'

'Or die trying!' Nancy whispered to Ellie after falling flat on her bottom six times in succession whilst trying to perfect her Yurchenko on the vault. 'He might not say it, but that's what he means!'

It was incredibly hard work and Ellie didn't think she'd ever ached so much in her life as she did by the end of her first week back at the Academy. But Oleg had a solution to that too. After their Friday training session, he called all the girls to the side of the gym, where they found a line of buckets waiting for them.

'Uh-oh,' whispered Nancy. 'What kind of torture has he got in mind now?'

'So, my cadets,' said Oleg, twirling his moustache as he spoke. 'In Romania we have ice bath in frozen lake after training session. It helps muscles heal more quickly, so gymnast can train longer and harder.'

'Is he saying he wants us to jump in a frozen lake?' whispered Kashvi, looking alarmed.

'Unfortunately, in England water is too warm – and anyway I not get permission.' Oleg looked disappointed but the girls all let out a sigh of relief.

'He was seriously thinking about dunking us in the boating lake, wasn't he!' whispered Nancy.

'So instead I bring frozen lake of Romania to the gym,' he said, triumphantly, waving at the line of buckets. 'These are full of ice!'

'And you want us to put our feet in them?' asked Bella.

Oleg nodded. 'And your hands.'

'Um – how long for?' asked Scarlett.

'Until you can no longer feel your fingers and toes,' said Oleg, cheerily. 'And then five minutes longer.'

'Brrrr!' said Camille. 'Won't we get frostbite?

'Or chilblains, or – just, like, lose the circulation in our toes!' added Nancy.

Oleg glared at her. 'No questions. No backchatting. Remember, your coach is like a god! You obey without question.'

Then he stormed off crossly, leaving the girls with no choice but to obey.

'We . . . n-n-need . . . to keep t-t-talking to distract us from the f-f-freezing pain!' said Nancy, her teeth chattering as she submerged her feet.

'S-so w-w-what exactly are we going to talk about?' asked Kashvi.

'How about the fact that S-s-sian Edwards and M-m-matt Simmons are dating?' said Kashvi.

'Who told you that?' said Nancy. 'No, let me guess. Robbie Sipson, right? Seriously, that boy is so annoying!'

'It is true,' said Camille. ''ow does 'e know everysing zat goes on?'

'Oh, he makes most of it up!' said Nancy. 'Do you know he told everyone Tam was kissing a girl in Development squad?'

'Seriously!' said Kashvi.

'But he's not – is he?' said Bella.

'Of course he's not!' Nancy snorted. 'It's just cos Katya keeps smothering him in kisses. Though I can't imagine why anyone would want to kiss my brother. It's just – eeuw!'

'Talking of Katya,' said Bella, 'what is she up to now?'

Ellie looked up to see where Bella was pointing. Katya had been working on the bars, where Sasha had been making her do basic circle-ups to improve her core strength. But she must have got bored because she was now walking along the top bar like she was on a tightrope.

'Wow!' said Nancy as Katya flipped backwards and landed on the lower bar without even a wobble.

'That move is definitely NOT in the rule book!' said Kashvi.

'Can it even be safe?' asked Bella, nervously.

'Not when Sasha catches her it won't be,' said Scarlett.

But Sasha was busy showing Lexi something on the beam and didn't glance up. Meanwhile, lots of the other girls in the gym had stopped what they were doing to watch and, realising she had a crowd, Katya started to show off, flipping herself backwards not once but twice and landing faultlessly on the lower bar again.

'Whoa! How does she do that?' said Nancy.

'It'll be her own fault if she falls and breaks a leg,' said Scarlett.

'Jealous, are we?' said Nancy, seeing the dangerous glitter in Scarlett's eyes. 'Cos she's got moves on the beam you can't even dream of!'

Scarlett went bright red, but she didn't get a chance to retort because just then Katya's performance was interrupted by a shout from below.

'Miss Popolova, *what* do you think you are doing?'

Sasha was standing by the pit, glaring up at Katya who slithered rapidly down to the ground, her eyes still bright with the thrill of performing.

'Do you realise how dangerous that manoeuvre is?' Sasha demanded.

'But I do it many time on high wire,' said Katya. 'Since was I little girl in Moscow.'

'You are not in Moscow now, Miss Popolova,' Sasha snapped. 'And this is not a circus. This is an elite gym and you are here to train.'

'But all I do is circle-ups, over and over,' Katya complained.

Sasha pursed her pink lips and spoke quietly. 'Bar is your weakest discipline, cupcake. You need to start at the beginning, just like everyone else.'

Katya shrugged. 'I know this,' she admitted. 'Only . . . sometimes I am getting a little bit . . . bored.'

'Training *is* boring sometimes!' Sasha said. 'To get to the top level is about repetition – pain – boredom. It's not about doing a few tricks to make people laugh.'

'OK. I will try not to do it again,' said Katya, unconvincingly.

'That's right,' said Sasha with a bright smile and a shake of her ponytail. 'Because if you break the rules again, I shall send you out of this gym quicker than you can say Chinese pole.'

'You know about Chinese pole?' said Katya, looking up hopefully.

'I was performing Chinese pole before you were

even born, Miss Popolova,' said Sasha. 'But right now we are in the gym, not the big top, and we are going to stick to gymnastics training and nothing else.'

Katya did not reply.

'You don't agree?' Sasha said. 'Well, if you can't commit to the boring bits of training, I'm afraid you don't get the privilege of the exciting bits.'

'I do not understand,' said Katya.

Sasha turned to all the other gymnasts. 'I wasn't going to tell you till later,' she announced, 'but Emma has invited Casey Cottrell to the gym next week, to help all the girls in Development and Pre-Elite develop new floor routines.'

'That must be the surprise Emma was talking about.' Nancy whispered.

Ellie grinned back happily. This was amazing news.

'Who is this Casey? asked Katya.

'She's only the best choreographer in the world!' said Lexi. 'She used to be a ballerina and then she switched to gymnastics.'

'She competed with Emma and Lizzie Trengilly in the Olympics!' explained Sasha. 'And now she coaches and choreographs.'

'And she will help us with our routines?' asked Katya, clapping her hands with excitement. 'I have lots of ideas –'

'Well, I'm afraid they will have to wait,' said Sasha. 'Because *you* won't be working with Casey.'

'But I have to,' said Katya. 'I need to . . .'

'First you need to learn that gymnastics is not a playground, cupcake,' said Sasha. 'The rules are in place for your safety. Because you have shown me that you are not prepared to obey the rules, you won't be working with Casey this visit.'

The gymnasts returned to training, but Ellie's stomach was full of excited butterflies as she thought about working with Casey. From the buzzy atmosphere in the gym she could tell the others were as thrilled as she was. Only Katya seemed quiet and subdued, working dutifully on easy but boring conditioning moves with a sulky expression on her face. Ellie felt sorry for her. Sasha had been really harsh. But then she thought about what might have happened if Katya had fallen, and shuddered. Sasha was right, of course. Safety had to come first in gymnastics, even if that meant the exciting stuff sometimes had to wait!

CHAPTER
Eight

For the next few days, all anyone at the Academy could talk about was Casey Cottrell. Famed for her incredible floor work, Casey had trained at the Royal Ballet School before switching to gymnastics when she was thirteen. She'd won individual gold on the floor in the Olympics then gone on to win World and European titles. Since retiring from gymnastics, she'd gained a reputation as one of the top choreographers in the country – and the world. And when Casey turned up at the gym the following Monday, the girls were not disappointed.

Casey was in her late twenties, stunningly

beautiful and incredibly sophisticated, with long
dark hair that fell down her back in waves.

'And she walks like ze prima ballerina too,' said
Camille with an envious sigh.

'She makes *everything* she does look like dancing,'
said Bella. 'I saw her drinking a cup of coffee with
Emma earlier, and she even made that look like a
scene from a ballet.'

'I am so sad I not work with her!' said Katya
plaintively.

Sasha had not relented, so Katya was the only
squad member who did not get to line up in front of
Casey at the beginning of the first session. Instead
she went to the far corner of the gym where Sasha
was making her work on boring bar repetitions.
Ellie couldn't help feeling desperately sorry for her.

'Hello, ladies,' said Casey, greeting them all with
a soft lilting Irish burr that couldn't have been more
different to Oleg's sergeant major bark. 'We're going
to start off this morning with a ballet lesson.'

'Sounds better than bootcamp,' whispered
Nancy. 'Although I'm not sure I'm the tutu type!'

'Then I'm going to work with each gymnast individually,' Casey went on, her voice so soft the gymnasts had to strain forwards to hear her. 'I want to find out all about your interests and your passions, so I can help devise a new piece uniquely suited to you.'

'Passions!' whispered Nancy. 'Doesn't she know I'm about as romantic as a brick?'

'I don't think she means *that* sort of passion!' giggled Bella.

'OK, so let's start with a warm-up – prima ballerina style!' said Casey.

Ellie loved the dance session. It was fun but challenging. After a fortnight of focusing on drills and technique, it made a refreshing change to work at the barre, pretending she was at the Royal Ballet, then try out hip-hop and street dance with a bit of ballroom and Latin thrown in for good measure. Casey encouraged them to have fun, to think about how to express themselves through dance.

After it was over, Casey took the girls off one by one to work with them in the little studio next to the gym. Ellie was surprised how nervous she felt when it was her turn, but Casey quickly put her at ease.

'You did well this morning,' she said, smiling at Ellie with a curious expression on her face – as if something about her was surprising, or unexpected. 'You like floor work, right?'

Ellie nodded. 'Floor and bars.'

'I should have known!' said Casey, with another smile that lit up her lavender blue eyes.

Ellie wondered what she meant, but Casey didn't give her chance to ask.

'OK,' she went on, sounding more businesslike now. 'You need to qualify at the Challenge Cup to get to Junior British Champs, right? So this routine is doubly important for you.'

Ellie nodded.

'And if you do qualify, you'll be going to British Champs virtually as an unknown.'

'I – I suppose,' said Ellie. She hadn't really thought about it before, but Casey was right. Apart from Team Champs, she'd never competed at a major national competition.

'It's pretty rare for a gymnast to come out of nowhere at the British,' said Casey. 'You won't be on the judges' radar and that automatically puts you at a disadvantage. So we need a routine to get you noticed.'

'By the judges?' said Ellie.

'Yes, and by the Team GB selectors.' said Casey. 'Barbara Steele will be there, and so will the other national squad coaches . . .'

Ellie shivered. The idea of being selected for the Junior GB squad felt like an impossibly far-off dream at the moment.

'. . . but most of all, you need to be noticed by the audience.'

Ellie was confused. 'I don't understand.'

'If the crowd go mad for a routine, the judges can see it's had an impact,' Casey went on. '*Then* they sit up and take notice!'

Ellie remembered how the others had been magnetically drawn to Katya as she tumbled across the bars. Despite the trouble she had got into afterwards, she'd definitely made an impact. Was that what Casey meant?

'Tell you what. Why don't you show me your old routine and we can go from there,' Casey suggested.

Ellie showed Casey the pirate-themed piece which Sasha had devised for her. She had always loved performing it because it reminded her of the cliffs and beaches and ocean views of her Cornish home. She quickly lost herself in the music, forgetting Casey was even watching as she let the memories soak over her. When the last chords sounded, she came back to reality with a jolt, suddenly feeling self-conscious. Casey stood there, saying nothing for what felt like forever.

'It's nice,' she said thoughtfully. 'Your music is very beautiful – the tumbling is great. And your dance elements are lyrical and graceful.'

'Is that – a good thing?' asked Ellie.

'It depends,' said Casey. 'If you were an established gymnast, probably. But I think you need to announce your arrival on the scene with more of a bang!'

'Um – how do I do that?' Ellie asked nervously.

'You need a routine that's edgy – shocking!' Casey smiled. 'A bit dangerous.'

Ellie felt uncomfortable. Oleg and Emma had told her to play it safe, but Casey seemed to be saying exactly the opposite.

'But isn't that risky?' Ellie asked. 'I mean – what if the judges hate it?'

'Love it or hate it,' said Casey with a smile, 'they won't be able to ignore it!'

For the remainder of the session, Casey made Ellie try out new things, asked her a lot of questions and made notes in a notebook. Ellie came away feeling as confused as ever.

Nancy felt the same way.

'Casey reckons I need a routine that reflects my soul,' she said that night, when the three girls were getting ready for bed. 'But I'm not sure there's anything very interesting in my soul. I mean, Ellie, you've got the creek, and Katya's got the circus . . .'

'But Casey doesn't like my creek routine,'

said Ellie. 'She thinks it's boring.'

'She didn't say that, did she?' asked Nancy.

'Not exactly, but I'm sure that's what she meant.'

'Well, I no work with Casey at all,' said Katya, who had been very quiet since they returned from the gym that day. 'Sasha make me work on bars all day long. I have to do easy things only.' She gazed up at the picture of her family that stood on the chest of drawers with a faraway expression on her face. 'Circle-up and shoot-up – baby moves, over and over.'

'It's cos you're so mega-bendy,' said Nancy.

'That's amazing for floor and beam,' added Ellie kindly. 'It's just that you need to learn to be more rigid for bars.'

'I know,' sighed Katya, tearing her eyes away from the photo. 'And I try, but was very hard for me when all I wanted was to come and dance with you.'

'It might not seem like it, but Sasha is really fair,' Ellie said with a smile. 'If you show her you can stick to the rules she'll stop being so hard on you.'

'No, she not like me,' said Katya, clambering into

her bed with a pout. 'But I will show her. I may have soul of circus girl but I have heart of gymnast too!'

'You see, everyone has an exciting soul except me!' wailed Nancy, flopping back on to the bed. 'I'm beginning to think mine must be empty.'

'Don't be daft – there's plenty in your soul,' said Ellie, smiling. The old bunk bed, which Nancy had just clambered into, was much too short for her now and when she stretched out, her long legs stuck comically out of the end.

'Like what?' asked Nancy.

'London, for a start,' said Ellie. 'The city must be part of who you are.'

'Not in the same way that the creek is for you,' said Nancy, wiggling her toes miserably. 'And, to be honest, sometimes I felt more at home in a boat in Cornwall than I ever have in London. The thrill of a rowing competition, the feel of the oars in my hands, rowing so hard it feels like my heart is going to come bursting out of my chest – it's amazing.'

Something about what Nancy was saying made Ellie feel a little uneasy. 'It sounds to me like your soul is a boat, Nancy,' she said firmly, climbing into bed and turning out the lamp. 'Best tell Casey and see what she can do with you!'

CHAPTER
Nine

'I've found you a piece of music that I think will suit you perfectly,' said Casey, when Ellie turned up for her session the next day. 'Listen!'

Ellie wasn't sure what she had been expecting, but it definitely wasn't this. The piece started quiet and simple, with sparse piano notes like raindrops, then suddenly it switched to high tempo hip-hop with an almost tribal drum beat. There was a crazy Charleston swing section, and then it finished with a wild war cry.

'It's great, isn't it!' said Casey.

'It's –' Ellie hesitated. 'It's really different to

what I've had before.'

'It's also totally different to what anyone else will be performing.'

'And that's good?' said Ellie, uncertainly.

'It's exactly what you need to get noticed,' said Casey. 'And I'm determined to make the world sit up and notice you, Miss Ellie Trengilly!'

Ellie nodded slowly. She appreciated what Casey was trying to do, but she just couldn't get her head round her new music. It wasn't a piece to get lost in. It certainly didn't feel like it reflected her soul – and the thought of performing to it made her feel completely terrified.

'I've taken a bit of a risk with the routine, as well,' Casey was explaining. 'There are some quite unusual moves – it's guaranteed to cause a stir.'

'Right . . .' Ellie tried to quieten the pulse of anxiety that was beating in her head.

'I promised to give you a moment in the spotlight,' said Casey. 'And this should do it!'

Ellie felt too nervous to properly take in what she was saying. 'OK – um – thanks.'

'So,' said Casey. 'Are you ready to start work?'

Over the next couple of sessions Ellie worked hard to learn Casey's new moves, and by the end of the week she had the whole routine down. And it was a great routine. Casey had put everything into it – but Ellie couldn't help thinking it would better suited to one of the other girls, like daring circus girl Katya or Kashvi, whose dances were lively and full of character. Or even Nancy, who was good at performing kooky funny jazzy pieces. But to Ellie it felt . . . uncomfortable. Showing off to the world just didn't come naturally to her. It felt like wearing someone else's clothes. They fitted fine but they didn't really suit her – and she didn't know how she could ever find a way to make them!

The other girls were all thrilled with their new routines. Kashvi's old Bhangra routine had been replaced with one inspired by urban skate culture, Camille's referred to the fashion world with catwalks and photoshoot moments, whilst Casey had devised a brilliant new piece for Nancy which nodded to her love of boats by using a nautical tune that Nancy said remi ided her of hanging out in Mr Trengilly's boatshed.

Only Katya had not been given one – and she was feeling very put out when she Ellie and the twins went to Mario's café for a Friday treat of hot chocolates.

Mario was the flamboyant Italian who owned the café in the park. The girls had befriended him last year, when they'd spend many happy afternoons practising tumbles by the boating lake. When he had been introduced to her, Mario had taken an immediate shine to Katya, and the little circus girl usually greeted him with a big hug. But today she was too despondent even to smile. When he brought over a tray of his famous hot chocolates, smothered with cream and marshmallows, she just looked up at him with sad puppy-dog eyes.

'What is the matter with you, little one?' Mario asked, his face clouded with concern.

'I am only girl in Academy with no floor routine,' said Katya sadly.

'And this is a bad thing?' asked Mario, confused. He wasn't exactly a gymnastics expert.

'She can't compete at Challenge Cup without one,' Nancy explained.

'Then you will get one!' said Mario. 'You must wait and see.'

'Sasha say she will make one for me if I stick to rules.' Katya admitted with a little pout.

'Well, that's great news!' said Tam, through a mouthful of cream and marshmallow. 'Don't worry. Sasha's a wonderful choreographer.'

'Yeah, different style to Casey, but great,' said Nancy.

'Maybe,' said Katya, but she didn't look convinced and even a nibble of a marshmallow failed to make her smile. 'But I do not think I will like a routine from Sasha.'

'Sasha devised my old routine and I loved it.' said Ellie, trying to cheer Katya up. Part of her still couldn't help wishing she could take her old sea-shanty piece to the Challenge Cup.

'But Sasha like you,' said Katya, mournfully. 'She

does not like me, and she does not like circus. She make me routine that is boring and no fun, I think.'

'If there's one thing Sasha Darling isn't, it's boring!' said Nancy.

'Now, if Oleg was devising your routine then you should be worried,' laughed Tam.

'Yes, he'd have you marching to army music or something,' said Nancy.

'But Sasha *will* come up with something brilliant,' Ellie reassured her.

'Maybe,' said Katya, 'but only if I do rules, and I am not a rules sort of girl!'

'I am thinking what you are needing is some chocolate fudge cake!' said Mario, hurrying off in the direction of the kitchen. 'I go get it - with ice cream, yes? No one can be sad with ice cream!'

'Thank you!' said Katya, managing a small smile. 'And I *have* found something that is me.' She pulled a flyer out of her pocket and waved it at the others. It had what looked like a circus tent on it - and a clown face in the corner. 'Is circus school not far from here!'

Tam reached for the leaflet, wiped away his hot-chocolate moustache and coughed theatrically before reading it out loud. 'Roll up! Roll up!' he declared and Katya giggled.

'Come and learn sensational circus skills,' Tam went on, 'tightrope to tumbling, aerial to acrobatics, clowning, juggling and much, much more, at the Sensational Circus Pocus. Beginners welcome!'

'Hey, that sounds epic!' said Nancy.

'So you will come with me?' Katya asked delightedly. 'You will love it! I promise you.'

Ellie's heart sank. There was no way the Academy would let them risk injuring themselves at a circus school. 'We can't!' Ellie looked at Nancy and Tam for support.

Tam nodded. 'We couldn't risk it, Katya. Not now, so close to a competition. And especially not Ellie and Nancy – they need to qualify, and so do you!'

'The coaches would go mad if they found out,' added Ellie. 'I could lose my scholarship. We could all get kicked out.'

'It does sound kind of cool though,' said Nancy, regretfully.

Ellie looked at her friend in surprise. Nancy gave a rueful shrug. Nancy almost sounded like she wanted to go.

'Yes, but they'd never allow it,' Ellie said.

'I understand. I do not want for you to get in trouble.' Katya said, looking sad and crushed all over again. She sighed. 'I will just find another way to bring fun to my gymnastics.'

Ellie gave her friend a big hug. 'Well, if you find a way, let me know too!'

CHAPTER
Ten

With the Challenge Cup just three weeks away, fun was something that Ellie couldn't really think about.

Oleg's insistence on perfection was definitely paying off. Ellie was making far fewer mistakes and she knew that her routines were more polished, more fluent than they had ever been. It was only her floor routine that still didn't feel right. She knew the tumbles were strong and all the other compulsory elements were virtually flawless, but she couldn't get her head around the dance elements. She knew she needed to be bolder, braver – to show off a bit – but that just didn't feel like her. And besides, it was hard to do all those things *and* concentrate on performing every skill with perfect ten precision.

'I'm just hoping I can get it right on time for Challenge Cup,' she confessed to Nancy as they pulled off their tracksuits in the gym for the beginning of an afternoon session.

'Of course you will,' said Nancy. 'And you're nailing really difficult skills, so you'll score high.'

'I hope you're right,' said Ellie with a sigh. 'And, hey, it's not long till Christmas. There's only one thing on my list for Santa this year.'

'Let me guess,' grinned Nancy. 'To ace the Challenge Cup and qualify for Junior British Champs while you're at it.'

'No, for us *both* to qualify,' said Ellie stretching out. 'And Katya too! She's being entered as well because she's so promising. You know, even though her bar is still really weak, she'll get massive scores on floor and beam to make up for it. I think she could do it.'

'It'd be cool if the two of you qualified together,' said Nancy.

Ellie turned to her friend in surprise. Nancy had seemed so relaxed about the competition recently. 'We're all going to!' she said firmly. 'You're looking great – your vault is explosive. Anyway, remember what Emma said about staying positive.'

'I'm not being negative, exactly.' Nancy shrugged. 'In fact, I'm way more chilled than I normally am before a competition. The way I see it, I'm lucky to have come this far. I've already come further than I ever expected!'

'You're talking as if it's all over after Challenge Cup,' said Ellie, looking anxiously at her friend who was staring down at her towel with a serious expression on her face. 'And it's not. After this, there's Junior British Champs, then Seniors, Europeans, Worlds, then who knows where.'

'Maybe,' said Nancy quietly. 'And if that happens, then great – I'll be thrilled, of course. But if I don't qualify at Challenge, then maybe it's time to think about whether gym is really what I want to spend my whole life doing.'

Ellie didn't know how to reply to that. She

wondered if she'd feel the same if she knew she'd never have a chance of competing on the national stage. Would she still want to do it? Somehow Nancy's resignation worried Ellie more than if she'd been having an attack of the nerves.

But just then Katya did something so shocking it made both girls forget what they'd been talking about. The small girl marched into the gym, went straight up to Sasha, stuck her hands on hips and announced loudly, 'I make my floor routine.'

The whole gym fell silent, stopped what they were doing and stared. Even the Elite squad were watching with interest.

Sasha did not reply. She simply raised a perfectly arched eyebrow.

'I tired of waiting,' Katya said. 'So I get music and I make my own routine.'

'Right,' said Sasha. Her pearly pink lips were set in a thin line.

'I look at rule book,' Katya declared. 'I include all the compulsory components. And I put in some of my own too.'

Ellie shifted awkwardly. Was Sasha going to explode?

But to her surprise Sasha only replied, 'Sounds like you've done your research, pumpkin.'

Katya looked a little bit nonplussed, as if she'd expected Sasha to argue with her too. 'Yes,' she said. 'I have.'

Ellie, who was sitting in box splits, glanced at Nancy and widened her eyes in surprise. 'I can't believe she made her own routine!' she whispered.

'I'm not sure it's going quite how she expected,' said Nancy, tugging her leg round so she was in the same position as Ellie.

'So,' Sasha went on. 'Can we see it?'

Katya looked a little thrown. 'Um – yes. I suppose.' Her voice sounded thin and reedy in the vast silent gym.

'Did you know about this?' Bella leaned over and whispered to Ellie.

Ellie shook her head. 'She was busy on the computer last night, but I thought she was just emailing her family or doing some homework.'

'She did ask me about ze components in my routine,' added Camille, who was stretching out her leg till it touched her head.

'Well, she's obviously done her research,' said Nancy. 'Can't wait to see what happens next!'

Katya had marched over to the sound system with a CD in her hand.

'You can only start one of your tumble sequences on two feet,' said Sasha. 'But I suppose you know that?'

'I know all rules,' said Katya defiantly, taking up her place on the floor.

'Great,' said Sasha, watching Katya intently, her eyes bright beneath her false eyelashes. 'Off you pop then, cherub.'

By now it wasn't just the gymnasts watching. Over by the door, Emma Bannerdown was also observing the whole scene with a quizzical look in her cool grey eyes.

When the music started, no one was surprised to see it was a circus themed piece – a little bit of clowning, a few showgirl moves – and also that

Katya's tumbling was electric. Ellie watched in admiration as she completed a full in back out – something she had only seen Sian Edwards do – before going on to do an Arabian double pike on the second. Katya beamed and wiggled and flirted with the audience, and she had studies – all the required elements were there. But still, Ellie couldn't help feeling that her routine was missing something, although she couldn't quite put her finger on what. Katya was clearly in her element performing to the crowd, though, and it was impossible to watch without smiling.

When Katya finished, the whole gym burst spontaneously into applause, but as Katya released her final pose, she only had eyes for Sasha.

There was a long pause, then Sasha gave a little shrug and said, 'Nice.'

'Just . . . nice?' said Katya, looking deflated.

'It showcases your skills pretty well,' Sasha said. 'And it doesn't break any rules. It should be fine.'

'Fine?' said Katya, her voice barely a whisper.

'I had actually devised a routine for you myself,'

said Sasha. 'I was going to help you work on it today, but I expect you'd rather stick with your own?'

'Whoah! I did not see that coming!' whispered Nancy.

'Neither did Katya,' said Kashvi, nodding at the younger girl.

Katya was no longer looking angry, or defiant – just crushed and a bit confused as she murmured, 'Um – I think – um – yes.'

'Her routine's great, though, isn't it?' asked Ellie.

'Yes, but I can't help wondering what Sasha's was like,' said Bella.

'I bet that's what Katya's thinking too!' said Nancy.

Camille shrugged. 'And now none of us will ever know!'

CHAPTER
Eleven

As the weather slid from golden autumn to damp cold winter, it became harder and harder for the gymnasts to drag themselves out of bed for the early morning sessions. It was dark when they made their way to the gym each morning and by the time they emerged in the evening, blackness had descended again. Nancy started to complain that she was suffering from light deficiency.

'I've forgotten what daytime even looks like!' she moaned, one particularly bleak day when thick fog made everything even gloomier than ever. Ellie found herself pining for the great outdoors too, and even Katya wasn't herself. Ever since her showdown with Sasha she had seemed subdued. Now she was working hard and sticking to the rules, but it was as if she had lost her circus sparkle in the damp English winter.

The next Sunday morning they all walked down to Mario's for hot chocolates and to get a change of scenery.

'Another date with your girlfriends, Tam?' said Robbie as they headed out the door of Head-Over-Heels House.

Tam rolled his eyes. 'Um – yeah, they're girls and they're my friends. Go figure!'

'If you say so, mate!' Robbie smirked.

Tam just shook his head and walked away, but Ellie could still hear Robbie laughing as they set off down the steps.

'I bet you can't wait to see your family at Christmas!' Ellie said to Katya as they made their way towards the park. Ellie was so excited about seeing her parents and sister and being by the creek again.

Katya's face fell. 'I not see them after all,' she said quietly.

'What?' said Nancy. 'I thought you were going back to Moscow after the Challenge Cup.'

'There is change of plan,' said Katya, her eyes suddenly bright with tears. 'I find out today that Popolov Circus will not be in Moscow – it is going to very far north of Russia. It would cost much money to travel, and take much time. I cannot go!'

Poor Katya looked so woebegone when she said this that neither Ellie nor Nancy could think of anything to say for a moment. 'What will you do?' asked Tam.

'I must stay in England,' said Katya with a dejected shrug.

'But Head-Over-Heels House will be shut up,' said Nancy. 'We're all going to Cornwall – even Mum.'

'I know!' said Ellie. 'It's obvious. You must spend Christmas with us!'

'Of course!' said Nancy.

Katya's tear-filled eyes lit up. 'But will there be space?'

'We'll make space!' said Ellie. 'My sister Lucy is dying to meet you. And Mum and Dad are totally relaxed about stuff like that. It'll be great fun!'

'We just need to get through the Challenge Cup,' said Nancy. 'And then Christmas will be here before we know it.'

When they got back from the café later, they found Head-Over-Heels House transformed into a winter wonderland. Sian and Sophia had decorated every inch of the house with tinsel, paper chains and fairy lights.

'It is so beautiful!' squeaked Katya, jumping up and down.

'Just do me a favour,' Tam said to the older girls, eyeing Katya warily. 'Promise me you'll keep her away from any mistletoe!'

The day of the Challenge Cup dawned bright and clear and Mandy drove the girls up in the Academy minibus, with Tam tagging along as their ever-loyal supporter. It was just the three of them going because all the other Academy gymnasts had already qualified for the British. They were meeting Oleg there, but Sasha was unable to make it because she'd come down with a flu bug.

Ellie privately wished her family could have been there. But Lucy had a ballet exam and Mum's new exhibition was opening in Truro that weekend – and anyway, there had been no money to spare for train tickets. Ellie no longer missed them as desperately as she had when she'd first come to London, but she still had days – like today – when she'd have done anything to have her family there supporting her. It made her wonder about her Aunt Lizze and what she was doing. If anyone could understand how she felt, it would be Lizzie.

They arrived at the venue to find Oleg wearing a shiny orange and grey tracksuit covered in a swirly pattern that Nancy said looked like her grandma's carpet. He had a huge smile on his face, and to their astonishment he grabbed all three girls, pulling them into a giant bear hug. 'My gymnasts! My gymnasts!' he declared, then he stood back and looked at them very seriously. 'Today you are my soldiers marching into war,' he declared. 'And I am your proud mamma, waving you off with a tear in her eye.'

'Did Oleg just say he was our mum?' whispered Nancy, trying very hard not to giggle.

Oleg released them and stood proudly to attention, his moustache quivering with emotion. 'Today you will execute your routines with such precision and grace that you will not give away a single deduction,' he declared. 'You will score perfect tens on every routine!'

'What exactly has happened to Oleg?' asked Nancy as the girls went off to get ready.

'He is in very good mood,' giggled Katya.

'Yeah, it's a bit freaky, isn't it!' said Ellie.

'Nothing can freak me out today,' said Nancy, with a grin. 'Look at me – I'm cool as a cucumber, calm as a carrot. I don't even know the meaning of nerves!'

'Good,' said Ellie. She hoped that Nancy's relaxed attitude was a good thing. 'Because you are going to ace this competition. We all are. We're the three Academy musketeers!'

CHAPTER
Twelve

Nancy's calm and confidence was clearly catching. Both Ellie and Nancy nailed their vaults with clean lines and sharp twists. They were perfectly on line in their landings, giving away barely any deductions. Nancy, too, performed a difficult double Yurchenko which earned her a really high difficulty score.

The bars, Ellie's strongest piece, went brilliantly. She was performing some very difficult skills but because she was so secure in her moves, she was able to focus on maintaining her rhythm and linking the individual skills together smoothly, making the bars do what she wanted and hardly giving any points away. It also helped to hear a familiar squeaky Russian voice rise clear from the other side of the auditorium. 'Come up, Ellie!' And then Tam's shout from up in the stands: 'She means come *on*, Ellie!'

The gymnasts' scores were brought to them by runners, little girls from a local gym club in silver dresses who delivered little slips of paper with each gymnast's score on it. A small girl with ginger hair in a tight bun brought Ellie's. She reminded Ellie of her sister Lucy, which made her smile.

'I've never seen anyone make the bars look like dancing before,' the little girl whispered as she handed over the score. 'It was wonderful.'

'Oh, thank you,' said Ellie.

'I want to be able to do that when I'm older,' she said as she ran off.

'So do I!' laughed Nancy.

'Hey – you just nailed a madly difficult dismount!' said Ellie, turning to her friend. 'And your vault scored way higher than mine. You're doing amazingly.'

'So's Katya,' said Nancy who seemed to be really

enjoying herself. 'Did you see her on the beam? And she's about to start on the floor now.'

Katya's floor routine was brilliant to watch, as always. The crowd were enthralled by her tumbling, and it was impossible not to smile at her cheeky little wiggles and flashy moments. Although Ellie still couldn't help feeling that the routine Katya had invented for herself didn't quite do her justice, there was no denying that it was a spectacular performance and the audience went wild for it. And wasn't that what Casey had told Ellie to do? Get the crowd on side and the judges would sit up and take notice.

And it clearly worked. Katya gave Ellie and Nancy a massive thumbs up when she received her score. But there was no time to ask what it was, because just then the judges announced that the warm-up period for the next rotation had begun.

Ellie always used to fear the beam because of the injury her Aunt Lizzie had sustained when she fell off it at the Olympic finals. She'd hurt her leg so badly that she could never compete again. That image rose in Ellie's mind now and she felt the familiar nerves rising in her stomach as she waited for the green light that was her signal to go. But this time Ellie let the weeks and weeks of precision training take over. She had practised them so much that the movements almost felt part of her, and when she dismounted and landed with a lightness she had rarely achieved before, she knew she had done well.

'You were amazing!' said Nancy, hugging her tightly when she rejoined her in the warm-up area, nearly squeezing all the breath out of her.

The runner handed her the score, and Ellie could hardly believe it. Her heart soared. She'd achieved a virtually perfect execution mark on beam. So far in the competition she'd scored 33.75, which meant she only had to get 12.25 on the floor to qualify. It wasn't a huge score. It was easily within her grasp . . . if only she could nail the new routine Casey had devised for her.

'Good start to the campaign!' Oleg beamed at the two girls. Nancy's competition was also still going well. She was on 32.65, not far behind Ellie. Both girls were within achievable distance of a score that could take them to Junior British Champs.

'It simple,' Oleg told them firmly. 'No mistakes on final rotation and you win this battle, easy peasy!'

'We just need to hold our nerve,' Ellie agreed as they left Oleg and made their way over to the floor for warm-up.

But when she glanced at her friend's face, she saw that something was wrong. 'Are you OK?' she asked.

Nancy shook her head. 'I feel sick!' she muttered.

'But you've done great so far. You're so close!'

'I think that's the problem,' said Nancy. 'Knowing I might be able to do it. I wasn't nervous before because . . . I'd given up hope.'

'I don't understand,' said Ellie. Time was running out. The warm-up had already begun. Oleg was helping Katya prepare for the vault – there was no one else around to help.

'I figured I was a lost cause,' said Nancy with a shrug. 'That's why I was so chilled. There's no point being nervous when you don't stand a chance, is there? But now – now I can see it's possible.'

'And that should give you hope!' said Ellie, frantically trying to take in what Nancy was saying.

'I just don't know if I want it any more!' said Nancy quietly.

'But isn't this your dream?' Ellie said. 'To go to the British, then Europeans, Worlds, the Olympics – go all the way.'

'It was,' said Nancy. 'It is . . . oh, I'm not sure. I just know that thinking this was my last competition was the only thing keeping me calm.'

Ellie took a deep breath and glanced over at Tam. He must be able to tell something was wrong – Ellie and Nancy weren't warming up. But because audience members weren't allowed to talk to gymnasts during the competition, there was nothing he or Mandy could do. It was down to Ellie to say the right thing.

She took a deep breath. 'You know what Emma would tell you,' she said gently. 'Just deal with one thing at a time. Don't think about the next competition. Just focus on your floor routine. Your beautiful rowing-boat floor routine that shows your soul, Nancy Moffat.'

Nancy had tears in her eyes. She gave Ellie the biggest hug. 'I guess you're right,' she said.

Ellie could feel Nancy trembling, so she hugged her back as tight as she could and whispered into her ear, 'Just do your best and then – well – we'll figure the rest out afterwards, OK?'

Nancy nodded and pulled away. Then, grinning through her tears, she said, 'OK, thanks, coach! Now forget about me and go wow the judges with that edgy routine of yours!'

Ellie didn't have the chance to warm up properly, or even get her head into gear before she heard her name being called. As she took her position on the floor, she knew she had to push all thoughts of Nancy out of her mind and try to recall everything that Casey had taught her. She had to own this routine, sell it to the audience, not let them see she was frightened of it.

The problem was that Ellie wasn't feeling very brave. Nancy's panic had unsettled her. She knew she needed to announce herself to the crowd – demand their attention – but she just couldn't do that right now. Her thoughts were elsewhere.

The routine didn't go badly. Ellie nailed the difficult tumbles, harnessing all her power to land each one confidently, and she found the bounce of the floor in her leaps and spins too. But she knew that her dance elements lacked conviction. The audience clapped her at the end, but they weren't cheering like they had for Katya and Ellie felt oddly flat as she walked off the floor.

'Don't beat yourself up!' said Nancy as she came off. 'You've definitely done enough to qualify.'

But Casey's words were finally starting to make sense to Ellie. The stakes were getting higher. Even if she qualified this time, Ellie knew in her heart that she would need something more at Champs. For now, though, she just needed to be there for Nancy.

'You can do it too,' said Ellie, giving her friend a hug.

'Maybe,' shrugged Nancy. She still looked frightened and shivery. 'We'll see.'

'You only need 13.35,' said Ellie. 'You've easily nailed that in practice before.'

But Nancy looked as pale as a ghost as she stepped up on to the floor, and as the music started Ellie could see she'd completely lost her nerve. She bungled her first dance moves and stumbled in her spin sequence. Then, just as she was about to launch into her tumble sequence, Nancy seemed to hesitate, as if she had forgotten completely what she was doing.

Ellie tried to send good luck vibes out across the blue floor but they didn't seem to be reaching Nancy. She landed outside the line on her first tumble sequence and the red flag went up. Nancy stumbled backwards and stuttered over her transition before launching into her next tumbling pass, over-rotating on her double back and landing flat on her bottom.

Ellie could see tears in Nancy's eyes now. She felt like crying herself as she watched her best friend make mistake after mistake.

In the audience, Tam was leaning forward, his face creased into a frown of concentration, his whole body tensed as if he wanted to be able to get up there and do it for his sister. Ellie had always known the twins were close, despite their constant play-fighting, but until that moment she'd never realised just how close they really were. Tam seemed to be feeling every tremor, every stumble Nancy made as if it was in his own body. Ellie didn't think she'd ever seen him look so desperate. He had once said that when he performed he calculated deductions in his head, 0.1 of a point off for a foot over the line, both feet over the line and you lost 0.3, a whole mark off for a fall, and Ellie was sure that was what he was doing now. With each mistake Nancy made there was another tenth deduction, and another, and another, until they all knew that thirteen or above was no longer a possibility.

There were tears flooding down Nancy's cheeks as she prepared to perform the final moves of her routine. It was heartbreaking to watch, and the whole crowd had fallen silent as if they were all feeling her pain, willing her to keep going.

And, funnily enough, Nancy performed the final

sequence utterly beautifully. Her face was creased in pain and she was still crying but she danced through those last few moments as if she was saying goodbye to the dream she'd been working towards for the past thirteen years. Ellie thought her heart might break as she watched her.

And then the music came to an end, the audience burst into applause in recognition of her bravery and Nancy crumpled to the floor. For a second she lay with her head in her hands, then she pulled herself up and flew straight into Ellie's arms.

'I blew it! I threw it all away!'

'You don't know,' said Ellie, holding her tight, trying to soak up her pain. 'Maybe it will still be enough.'

But they both knew it wasn't. They knew even before the runner came with the slip that there was no way Nancy could possibly have scored over thirteen.

The little girl with the ginger hair who had spoken to Ellie earlier handed Nancy her slip and said, 'You were so brave, the way you carried on.'

'Thank you,' said Nancy, taking the piece of paper but not opening it. Then she turned to Ellie and said, 'Hey, if one of us was going to do it, I'm glad it was you.'

'Neither of us knows anything for sure yet,' said Ellie. She had been so focused on watching Nancy that she was only dimly aware that a runner had pressed a slip of paper into her hand too. She looked down at it now, realising it contained her whole future, and her stomach clenched.

'Let's open them together,' said Nancy.

'Together,' said Ellie. And she put her arm around her dearest friend in the world and they both opened their slips at the same moment.

'11.225,' said Nancy as she unfolded hers. 'Well, that's it then.'

'Oh, Nancy, I'm so sorry.'

'Never mind,' said Nancy, wiping tears from her eyes. 'Come on – what does yours say?'

Ellie had been staring at her own piece of paper without taking it in. The little numbers seemed like a jumble. 'I – I don't know.'

'Give it here.' said Nancy. Then she shrieked with excitement and started jumping up and down. '13.95! 13.95! You did it, Ellie. You did it! You qualified. You're going to Champs!'

And then Nancy was hugging Ellie and they were both laughing and crying at the same time and Ellie hardly even knew how she felt any more. She was going to Junior British Champs – all her dreams were coming true – but she was going without Nancy. She was going without her best friend. Her heart was bursting with relief whilst Nancy's must be breaking into a million pieces.

And Ellie realised something at that moment. If she had the chance to go to the British and Nancy didn't, then she owed it to her friend to give it everything, hold nothing back. She was going to have to take a risk, and all of a sudden she knew what that risk would have to be.

CHAPTER
Thirteen

Nancy went to see Emma the day after the Challenge Cup to discuss her future. Nancy had gloomily predicted that Emma would kick her out of the Academy, but things didn't turn out that way.

'She actually said she had faith in me,' said Nancy, as the twins, Katya and Ellie sat round the kitchen table at Head-Over-Heels House discussing it that evening, 'and that I can always try to qualify again next year if I want to. She said I should go away over Christmas and think about it.'

'That's great news,' said Ellie. 'Isn't it?'

'I guess so,' Nancy shrugged. 'I don't know.'

They all fell silent for a moment, and then Tam quickly declared, 'What we need is to get your bum on a boat, Nancy Moffat.'

Nancy laughed and punched her brother on the arm. 'Cheeky!'

Over the past twenty-four hours, Tam had shown how well he knew Nancy. Instead of being sympathetic, he'd teased her mercilessly about crying during her routine and made her laugh with his impressions of her snivelling somersaults. It was exactly what she needed.

And Nancy had showed her incredible strength of character. She had congratulated Ellie and Katya and insisted that they celebrate their success and forget about her disappointment.

Because, amazingly, Katya had managed to achieve a qualifying score too. Only just – she shaved in on 46.2, just 0.2 points over the necessary total. But it was enough. Her bar work had been weak but her astonishing tumbling and beam work had more than made up for it. Despite only being at the Academy for a term, she was going to British

Champs – it was an incredible achievement!

'Rowing does sound like a plan,' said Ellie. 'Nobody can be miserable on the creek. Plus, Dad's had a brilliant idea!'

The others looked at her expectantly.

Lucy had told Ellie about it the previous night. 'He's converted the boatshed for us to sleep in. It'll be like camping, only in with all the old rudders and boaty bits and bobs.'

'Wow!' said Nancy. 'That'll be cool!'

'It'll be way more than cool – it'll be freezing!' said Tam, pretending to shiver. 'I mean, there's no heating in the boatshed, is there?'

'Nope,' said Ellie. 'And the weather forecast is for snow over Christmas. Mum said we all need to bring our thermals!'

'Katya, you're gonna love it!' said Tam. 'The sub-zero temperatures will make you feel like you're in Russia for the holidays!'

'Of course she'll enjoy it,' said Nancy. 'Sand, sea, snow and Santa – what more could anyone ask for?'

Ellie smiled. There was one more thing she knew

she had to ask for before the Christmas holidays arrived.

Ellie didn't know if Tam would even have the circus leaflet any more but he admitted to having kept it in his bag the whole time. 'I thought you might ask,' he said. 'Just be careful, yeah?'

When Ellie suggested her idea to Katya, though, she could hardly speak at all, she was so excited. 'You won't regret coming to circus – I promise!' she breathed, her eyes sparkling.

'I reckon it's something we both need,' Ellie admitted. 'I'm just sorry it took me so long to figure it out.'

Ellie had finally realised that if she was ever going to give a performance with wow factor she needed lessons from the best performer she knew – Katya. She knew it was a massive gamble, but Ellie had decided it was worth it. If she was caught, she might lose her scholarship, or even get kicked out – but if she didn't do something . . . well, she might never progress anyway. So it had to be worth it . . . it just had to.

Katya and Ellie made the short bus ride together to the old Victorian warehouse where the school was run together, one Sunday just before the end of term. The circus school didn't look particularly exciting from the outside, but Ellie gasped when they stepped through the door. High brick walls towered up to metal girders, and giant curved glass windows cast dusty shafts of sunlight across the massive room. Brightly coloured equipment was clustered at the edge of the room – ribbons and juggling balls, stilts, a board for throwing knives at – and hanging from the ceiling were trapezes, long lengths of blue silk and tightropes stretched across from one side of the hall to the other. Ellie watched in amazement as a young man pedalled a unicycle slowly across a tightrope whilst a girl span from a hula hoop ten of feet off the ground.

'Wow!' she breathed.

Just then, a man dressed in large baggy clown trousers and giant oversized shoes somersaulted across the floor, coming to a stop in front of them and bowing low. His face was free of make-up but he sported a giant nose and a big floppy hat which he swept off as he greeted them, only to reveal a baseball cap underneath it.

'Howdy, folks!' he said in a strong American drawl as he tugged off his nose to reveal a weathered but kindly face underneath. 'I'm Harry the Hat, or just Harry to you. You come to check out Circus Pocus?'

'Yes,' said Ellie shyly. 'We've come from the London Gymnastics Academy.'

'Is that so?' said Harry, looking at them both with interest. 'We get lotsa gymnasts joining the circus – overlap, you know!'

'It's true,' declared Katya proudly. 'I am from circus, from Popolov Circus in Moscow. My name is Katya Popolova, and my father is owner.'

'You kidding me?' said Harry the Hat. 'Your daddy is one of the greatest in the business.'

Katya beamed happily. 'You know my father?'

'And that somersaulting granny of yours! Any Popolova is always welcome at Circus Pocus,' said Harry, extending a gloved hand towards Katya, who shook it enthusiastically. He looked at Ellie. 'And you are . . .?'

'Ellie.'

'Ellie, you're also welcome to come along any time you like – no charge.'

Ellie remembered Katya saying that the circus was like one big family – and it seemed like she was now part of it! She looked round at the equipment. She was longing to have a go at juggling or tightrope walking!

Harry caught her looking. 'Go ahead and try anything you like. We're usually pretty quiet on a Sunday. Just a few regulars, plus me and my gal over there.' Harry waved up towards the ceiling where the hula hoop girl was now twisting around on a length of silk like a fish dancing in the waves. 'Hey, Dee Dee, come down and let me introduce you to my new acquaintances.'

The girl slid down the silk like a spider from its web. She was wearing an old pair of leggings and a tatty vest top, but she still managed to look incredibly beautiful. She had large black eyes, olive

118

skin and bright red hair that was twisted into dozens of snake-like tendrils that stuck up all over her head. When she spoke she had the same cowgirl drawl as Harry.

'Hey there!' she said. 'Welcome to Circus Pocus. You come to learn to fly?'

'You can teach us to do that?' said Ellie, gazing up at the silk.

'Sure!'

'But, I mean – it looks a long way to fall.' Suddenly, Ellie felt her fears coming back. She was risking so much by being here – what if she did injure herself and couldn't compete? Was it really worth it?

'Don't worry – we'll fit you with safety harnesses to start with,' said Harry. Dee Dee was looking at Ellie curiously.

'Say, don't I know you?' she asked.

'Um – I don't think so.' Ellie thought she would definitely remember meeting this extraordinary woman who looked like a cross between a pirate princess and Medusa.

'You sure do look familiar.' Dee Dee shook her

119

head, looking puzzled. 'Well, never you mind. I'll figure it out. Come on then – let's show you the tricks of the circus, kiddos!'

CHAPTER
Fourteen

Ellie quickly forgot all her fears in the magical atmosphere of Circus Pocus. Dee Dee showed her how to use the silks and the tightrope and Katya tried to teach her juggling, which she just couldn't get the hang of!

Ellie found it exhilarating. After weeks of playing it safe in Oleg's training sessions, it was liberating to try new things and test her body to the limit. She forgot all her worries about breaking the rules – or her bones – as she immersed herself in the world of the big top.

And it was astonishing to watch Katya in her

home environment. She was so alive, so full of crazy energy that Ellie wouldn't have been surprised if sparks had come flying out of her. 'You're fizzing like a firework up there!' she laughed as Katya flew past, flinging herself off a trapeze and flipping mid-air before catching hold of the other trapeze as it swung past. It was sort of like the uneven bars – if they were twenty metres up in the air and constantly in motion. Ellie couldn't understand how Katya found the bars so difficult if she could do this. She wondered if there was a way to help Katya work out how to transfer her amazing trapeze skills to the bars.

Katya finally descended from the trapeze, looking happier than Ellie had seen her for weeks, and dragged Dee Dee over.

'Dee Dee knows my mother,' she said excitedly. 'And she says she knows your family also, Ellie!'

'My family?' Ellie felt puzzled. 'But they're not circus people.'

'You looked so familiar when you first walked in,' said Dee Dee, grinning at Ellie. 'Then Katya told me your last name and I figured out why. You look just like Lizzie – absolutely the spitting image of her.'

'Oh, you mean my aunt.' Ellie felt embarrassed. She was so proud of Lizzie, but sometimes she wished her name didn't carry quite so many expectations.

'Oh yeah! You got that same way of talking that she has,' said Harry, who had come over to join them, his big clown shoes replaced by a pair of tatty Converse. 'And the same way of tipping your head on one side when you're thinking. I shoulda guessed who you were at once.'

'What? You've actually *met* her?' Ellie said in surprise.

'Met her in China last summer, didn't we, Dee?' said Harry. 'They're setting up a big new circus out there, Las Vegas style. Lizzie was training their acrobats.'

'Wow, that's . . .' Ellie could hardly believe it. Aunt Lizzie had never been particularly good at keeping in touch – the odd postcard from a far-flung location, occasional emails when she chanced across an internet café. As far as everyone knew, she'd given up on gymnastics for good. But now Harry was saying Lizzie was involved in the circus?

'Was she performing?' Ellie asked, confused.

'No, she was coaching,' said Dee Dee. 'Darn good coach she made too.'

'I did not know your aunt was in circus, Ellie,' Katya said, looking at her friend curiously. 'Maybe we get a message to her? She would want to know that you go to the British Championships, no?'

'I'm afraid I don't know where she is now,' Dee Dee said, looking at Ellie sympathetically. 'China was last autumn.'

Ellie couldn't help thinking that if Lizzie had been interested at all she would have already been in touch. Looking at Dee Dee's expression, she could tell she was thinking the same thing. Ellie felt a sudden rush of sadness and longing for the aunt she barely knew – who didn't seem to want to get to know her at all!

*

When Ellie and Katya got back to Head-Over-Heels House the first person they bumped into was Scarlett.

'Where have you two been?' she demanded, taking in their flushed faces and chalky work-out kit. 'And *what* have you been doing?'

'Nowhere' said Ellie quickly, aware of colour flooding into her cheeks.

'Nothing,' said Katya squeakily.

'Well you've been *nowhere* for ages,' said Scarlett narrowing her eyes suspiciously. 'And you both look too hot and bothered to have been doing *nothing*.'

'Sorry, gotta dash,' said Ellie, grabbing Katya's hand and dragging her upstairs to their room before Scarlett could ask any more questions.

Nancy and Tam joined them a few minutes later. Ellie flicked on the computer and pushed away thoughts of Scarlett as Katya filled the twins in on what they'd found out from Harry and Dee Dee. She typed in the name of the Chinese circus Harry had mentioned, along with the name Lizzie Trengilly, and sure enough, Lizzie's name popped up. There were lots of indecipherable entries in Chinese, but there was also a piece from the *New York Times* which talked about former Olympic gymnast, Lizzie Trengilly, helping to train the next generation of circus stars.

'How old is your aunt?' asked Katya, looking at the picture of Lizzie outside the big top. 'She looks so young.'

'She's only twenty-seven,' said Ellie. 'She's my dad's baby sister.'

'What's she up to now?' asked Tam.

Ellie shook her head. The piece was dated September that year and didn't really tell them anything that Harry hadn't. Until Nancy noticed the final paragraph.

'Look,' she said. 'It says here that Casey Cottrell was there too – that they helped choreograph the show together.'

'Wow,' said Tam. 'So Casey was working with your aunt a few months ago.'

'And she never mentioned it to you the whole time she was at the Academy,' said Nancy. 'That's weird!'

Ellie remembered some of the things that Casey had said that she hadn't understood at the time. She'd been so wrapped up in worrying about her floor routine she hadn't thought to ask what Casey had meant – but now she thought about it, they had been really odd.

'Maybe Casey thought you already knew,' said Tam, as if he could read her thoughts.

'How annoying!' said Nancy. 'You could have asked her a ton of questions about Lizzie.'

'And now I won't get chance to,' sighed Ellie. 'Because Casey's gone off to California, and she won't be back in England until the British.'

It was hard not to feel hurt by how difficult her aunt was making it for Ellie to ever reach her. It would have been amazing to talk to someone about her hopes and fears for her gymnastics career – now more than ever.

But then Ellie caught Nancy looking at her and felt awful. Nancy was the one who had real worries, and after a day at the circus Ellie was feeling happier than she had for ages. In fact, she couldn't help smiling as she remembered the freedom she'd felt, like she'd been sprinkled with magic circus dust, transformed for just a few moments into a star of the big top. And, who knew, if she could hold on to that feeling – it might be just what she needed to make her floor routine shine!

CHAPTER
Fifteen

Ellie didn't think she'd ever been so happy to be going back to the creek. Winter in London was so cold and damp and drizzly that Ellie had missed the seaside more than she had ever done. The low winter skies made her pine for the wide-open ocean vistas of home. Mandy drove Ellie, Katya and the twins on the long journey from London down to deepest darkest Cornwall in the Academy minibus.

Trengilly Cottage was on the Helford River, on a little tidal estuary with its own beach and spectacular views out over the water. As they rounded a corner and caught their first sight of the river through the bare hedgerows, Ellie felt her heart lighten. The creek was looking more beautiful than she'd ever seen it. The falling winter light was white-gold on the frost-laden trees, and the water glistened in a silver sheet like a mirror. Ellie breathed in the frosty air and felt something deep inside her relax like it always did when she came home.

But there was no time to take in the views because Mum, Dad and her sister Lucy were waiting for them on the steps of Trengilly Cottage. As soon as Ellie clambered out of the minibus, she found herself being enveloped in hugs from three directions at once.

'I've missed you all so much!' she said breathlessly.

'We're so glad you're here,' said Lucy, her face pink and happy under her cloud of red hair. 'I've been watching out for you for the past two hours. I thought you were never going to come!' Ellie put her arm around her happily.

'The minibus didn't much enjoy the tiny winding country lanes!' laughed Mandy.

'Sometimes road is so thin, we think bus going to

get stuck forever,' said Katya and everyone laughed.

'Lucy, Mum, Dad, this is Katya Popolova,' said Ellie, keeping her arm around her sister as she introduced her new friend.

'Oh, we've been dying to meet you,' said Lucy to Katya, her eyes shining. 'Ellie's talked about you so much and I want to know all about the circus!'

'And I want to see boathouse we sleep in,' said Katya. 'I still no understand – are we sleep inside the boats – on water?' She glanced suspiciously at the creek as if the idea didn't appeal to her one bit.

'No,' laughed Lucy. 'Come on, I'll show you!'

Ellie gave her parents another brief hug, then followed her sister, who was already dragging Katya and the twins to see their boatshed Christmas campsite.

'Look!' Lucy said, beaming excitedly as she pulled open the boathouse doors. 'Mum and I spent ages trying to make it cosy. Do you like it?'

Ellie barely recognised her Dad's workshop. Mum had draped gauzy fabric from the ceiling to create the effect of being inside a tent, Lucy had covered the whole thing with fairy lights, and there were makeshift beds laid out on the floor, each with a sign painted with the name of the occupant.

'Ellie, you're sleeping next to me,' said Lucy. 'Because I missed you so much it hurts!'

Ellie smiled and gave her little sister another big hug. She didn't think she'd ever been so happy to see her.

'And Katya's on the other side of me.' Lucy grinned and so did Katya. Ellie had a feeling the two of them were going to get on like a house on fire.

'I love it,' said Katya, waving her arm around. 'Remind me of sleeping in big top!'

'That's what we hoped!' grinned Lucy, happily. 'Nancy's by Ellie, of course. And Tam, you're next to the door. So if any sea monsters come and try to eat us then you can protect us.'

'Or they can eat him first,' said Nancy. 'Then decide he's disgusting and leave the rest of us alone.'

'Thanks, sis,' said Tam with a grin.

'So when do we get to go out on the water?' asked Nancy, throwing her rucksack down on to her sleeping bag and glancing around as if she was trying to work out where Mr Trengilly had hidden the boats. 'I'm dying to take *Jorian* or *Roo* out for a spin.'

'I knew you'd say that!' said Lucy. 'Dad and I managed to borrow a couple of extra life jackets – although they are a bit old and mouldy smelling.'

'A bit like Nancy,' said Tam, quick to get back at his sister for her monster comment.

'I don't care if they stink to high heaven,' said Nancy. 'I just want to feel the waves rocking beneath me.'

'Come on then,' said Lucy. 'Let's hit the creek!'

They spent a brilliant afternoon messing about in the boats. Nancy looked happier than she had in weeks, while Tam – who was a terrible sailor – lay back and let her do all the rowing, shouting out instructions every now and then. 'Although if I actually listened to you we'd end up stuck in the bushes,' Nancy pointed out. 'Or at the bottom of the creek!'

Meanwhile, Lucy and Ellie attempted to coax Katya into having her first rowing lesson. But the usually fearless Katya Popolova was not to be persuaded. She stared at the boat and the water as if they were wild beasts that might devour her.

'I no like water,' she said, her face set in the same determined pout that she'd worn when she was taking on Sasha.

'But, Katya, you fling yourself through mid-air on the trapeze,' said Ellie. 'How can you be frightened of a little rowing boat?'

'What if there are sharks – or octopuses?'

'There are no sharks or octopuses in the creek,' laughed Ellie.

'Still, I stay on land,' Katya declared.

'Maybe you'd feel safer in a big boat,' said Lucy. 'I could ask Dad to take us out in *Diablo*. That might help build up your confidence.'

'Yes, big boat,' said Katya decisively. 'Little small boat like this is not good at all for me! I am not having sea toes.'

'Fine!' said Lucy. 'But by the end of this holiday,

I promise you'll have found your sea toes – and your legs and arms too!'

Everyone laughed and Ellie looked round at the beach and the creek, where all her best friends in the whole world were gathered, and felt sure that this was going to be the best Christmas ever.

CHAPTER
Sixteen

That night they camped out in the boathouse, which was just as cold as Tam had predicted it would be. Nancy wore six pairs of socks, three jumpers and two pairs of jogging bottoms, and Tam insisted on wearing a funny green bobble hat that Nancy reckoned made him look like a weird kind of caterpillar when he stuck his head out of his purple sleeping bag.

Katya felt right at home in the cold, declaring that in Russian winters the temperatures fell far lower. But she snuggled her sleeping bag close to Lucy, with whom she had already struck up a great friendship, and the two whispered and giggled for what seemed like hours before they finally drifted off to sleep.

Ellie loved falling asleep to the sound of the waves lapping on the shore and the seagulls calling overhead. She dreamt of performing her new routine on the beach, so vividly that she could almost feel the sand between her toes. In the dream, her routine seemed to work. She performed it to the trees and the waves and the gulls that looped and soared above, and she felt as if she made it her own in a way she'd never managed in the gym.

When she woke, everything felt different somehow. She could hear the sound of the water but it was muffled, eerily distant, as if somebody had thrown a blanket over it. Taking care not to wake the others, Ellie wriggled out of her sleeping bag and tiptoed towards the entrance. Shivering in the early morning chill, which seemed even colder than it had last night, she pulled open the door and was confronted with a sea of white.

The beach was no longer visible under a thick

layer of white powdery snow, and the sky was a brilliant blue against which the trees stood out as white silhouettes. Even the creek itself seemed to be a different colour as it reflected the frozen scene.

It was so beautiful that Ellie couldn't help smiling. She pulled on her wellies which were standing by the door and tugged on her coat over her pyjamas before stepping outside and pulling the shed door closed behind her. Her feet made a muffled crunching sound as she stepped out into the silent morning.

'Please don't tell me you're going to try doing a round-off in this!' said a voice from behind her.

Ellie turned to see Tam emerging from the boatshed too. Still in his pyjamas and wearing wellies, one of Dad's fisherman's jumpers and his green bobble hat, he looked dead silly. But she probably looked the same.

'I *was* just wondering if gymnastics in wellies was possible,' she admitted.

'Well, there's only one way to find out,' said Tam with a grin.

The beach looked so perfect – an untouched sheet of white, like a blank canvas. It was almost too good to resist.

'I'm up for it if you are!" said Ellie, taking a deep breath before attempting a running somersault. But it was almost impossible to run properly, let alone get any elevation and she landed in a snowdrift. She stood up laughing and wiping snow out of her eyes. 'Come on, Tam! Your turn.'

Tam tried a handspring, sending snow flying everywhere – along with one of his wellies. He landed in the snow and when he sat up he looked more like a snowman than a gymnast.

'Gymnastics in wellies – not so good!' he laughed, picking himself up and shaking like a dog to get the snow off him.

Ellie stood up and tried to plough a round-off flick through the powdery white. She managed to land it this time, but then immediately toppled backwards, almost falling on top of Tam.

As they lay there catching their breath, Tam said, 'I didn't get chance to thank you.'

'What for?'

'For looking after Nancy at the Challenge Cup.'

Ellie sat up and shook snow out of her hair. 'If I'd done a better job she might have qualified.'

'At least you cared enough to try,' said Tam. 'You risked your own competition for her – you could have messed up your floor routine without a warm-up.'

Tam's dark hair was flecked with snow and there were even flakes on his lashes. Ellie sighed. 'My floor didn't exactly go so great anyway.'

'Your routine's great!' said Tam. 'You just need to show it off more. Do you think going to the circus will help?'

'I hope so,' said Ellie. 'I feel really bad lying to everyone else about it, though.'

'If it works, it's got to be worth it.' Then Tam grinned. 'You know what you really need, right? To give it a bit more welly!'

'Welly?'

'Yup. Like this!' Before Ellie knew it, Tam had retrieved his lost wellington and emptied its snowy contents all over Ellie's head.

'Hey – that's cheating!'

The other girls emerged from the boatshed to find Ellie and Tam, covered in snow, lying in a heap and laughing uncontrollably.

'Ooh – it remind me of home!' said Katya, taking in the snowy scene with bright-eyed amazement.

'Well looks like there's only one thing for it,' said Nancy. 'Snowball fight!'

The next moment they were all throwing snowballs in every direction, shrieking, ducking, lobbing and diving. By the time they made their way up to Trengilly Cottage half an hour later they all looked like snowmen, and Mum and Mandy both shook their heads in despair as they trooped through the door, scattering snow everywhere.

But soon their wet clothes were hanging up on every available surface of the kitchen and the five of them were sitting in front of the fire, with mugs of hot chocolate and plates of toasted teacakes covered in dripping melted butter.

'Mmm – I love being really, really cold and then warming up again!' said Ellie.

'I just love these teacakes!' said Tam.

'And I can't wait to get back out on the water again today,' said Nancy. 'I've been dreaming of boats for weeks.'

'So have I,' said Tam. 'Only mine are usually nightmares in which I capsize.'

'Those aren't dreams – that's real life!' said Nancy. 'You are the world's worst sailor!'

'Well, if you want a taste of the water you can all come out with me today,' said Dad, appearing at the door. 'I've got to pick up the Christmas supplies – the turkey and all the trimmings – but the roads are impassable, so I'm going to take *Diablo* round the coast. It's the only way to get to the supermarket today.'

'You go shopping in boat?' asked Katya, looking puzzled.

'It's actually quicker than by road,' Lucy explained. 'We do it all the time.'

'So, who's in?' asked Dad.

Everyone put their hands up in the air – except Katya.

'Oh, come on!' pleaded Lucy. '*Diablo* is steady as rock.'

Katya still looked unconvinced.

'We can visit my old gym whilst we're in town,' suggested Ellie.

'Hmm,' Katya frowned. 'This *Diablo* boat is big and not rocky rolly, you say?'

Lucy nodded.

'OK – I try,' she said. 'But if I drown, I will be very cross!'

Lucy giggled. 'Then we promise not to let you do any drowning, OK?'

CHAPTER
Seventeen

So, half an hour later, the five of them – plus Dad – piled into *Diablo*. They were wrapped up in as many layers as Mum and Mandy could talk them into and bundled in the odd assortment of life jackets Lucy had begged or borrowed for their stay.

Katya was looking decidedly green.

'You can walk a tightrope and somersault on to a horse's back,' said Lucy. 'How can you be afraid of a boat?'

'Boats are much more frightening than tightrope or trapeze!' said Katya. 'What if we are getting lost out at sea? And shipwrecked?'

'Don't worry. Dad knows these waters like the back of his hand,' said Ellie. 'He could navigate them blindfold if he had to.'

Luckily no blindfold was required. The day was as crisp, bright and beautiful as Ellie thought a Christmas Eve should be. And as *Diablo* took off from the pontoon and headed out from the little back waterways of the creek into the open river of the estuary, they could see the ocean ahead, light sparkling on the waves. While they were in the estuary, *Diablo* felt like quite a big boat, but as they passed the headland and went out on to open water it was a different matter. Against the backdrop of the wide horizon she seemed tiny. Even on a calm windless day the water was still choppier out in the ocean, causing the boat to bob around, rising and falling on the crest of the waves.

'You say water will be flat as pancake!' said Katya, looking accusingly at Lucy.

'This *is* really calm, honestly!' laughed Lucy.

'Stare at a fixed point,' suggested Ellie. 'Like in gymnastics when you're doing a turn. That keeps your stomach steady.'

Katya groaned. She was white as a sheet and clinging on to the side of the boat. Nancy, on the other hand, was pink cheeked and looked more alive than Ellie had seen her in months. Dad let Nancy take the helm and she navigated *Diablo* through the surf like she'd been doing it for years, wind sweeping her hair backwards, her eyes alight.

This was exactly what Nancy needed, Ellie thought to herself. She caught Tam's eye and knew he was thinking the same thing.

Despite Katya being convinced they were all going to drown, they made it safely into the old town harbour, moored the boat up against the giant stone quay and clambered up the metal ladder on to dry land.

'I never going to step foot into boat again!' Katya declared firmly.

'I'm afraid you'll have to step your foot in one more time if you want to get back home,' said Dad. 'But after that we promise to keep you on dry land! Now, I'm going to pick up the Christmas provisions.

I'll meet you folks back here in a couple of hours, OK? No longer than that, or we'll miss the tide.'

'What this mean?' asked Katya.

'Oh, the creek's tidal,' explained Ellie. 'At low tide there's no water in it, which means we can't get the boat back to the cottage.'

'We'd have to wait twelve hours for the next high tide,' Lucy added.

'We'd be stuck out at sea for Christmas Day!' said Nancy cheerily, as if she quite liked the idea.

'OK, best not be late then!' said Tam. He didn't share Nancy's enthusiasm for Christmas on the waves.

While Dad went to the supermarket, Ellie took the others up the hill to her old gym, where Lucy still trained. They weren't surprised to find it open on Christmas Eve. 'Gymnastics is a twenty-four seven, three hundred and sixty-five day a year sport,' said Tam. 'Or maybe three hundred and sixty-four. We get Christmas Day off to stuff ourselves full of turkey and pudding, and then it's back to conditioning on Boxing Day!'

'You say that like it's a good thing!' said Nancy.

'It is,' said Tam. 'More than one day off gym and I get withdrawal symptoms.'

Ellie felt just as Tam did, that a day without gymnastics was a day wasted. It was wonderful to be back in her own gym and see her old coach, Fran. Fran let them work on their own whilst she coached a group of nine-year-olds. The younger girls watched the older gymnasts with shining eyes, but Ellie only had eyes for Lucy – and she was amazed by the progress she'd made. She had changed over the last year. Her figure had become stronger and more toned and her crazy exuberance was now tempered with a quiet determination that Ellie didn't think she had seen there before.

'I'm doing more hours since I passed Grade Four,' Lucy explained when they went for a drinks break. 'Fran reckons I need to build up my strength if I want to get into the Academy. Mum still says she's no idea how they'll afford it if we both go, but Dad says he'll think of something.'

Ellie frowned. She was worried about that too.

But then she said quickly, 'Of course we'll think of something. The Trengillies always do!'

'I read in *Gymnast* magazine that GB squad members get extra funding,' said Lucy. 'So when you nail it at Junior British Champs and get selected for national squad, that'll help loads!'

'*If* I get selected,' said Ellie, with a sigh. If only the secret circus sessions could do the trick, give her the edge, help her get selected – then her family's money worries might be over!

'Well if you go in with that attitude, you've failed before you started,' said Nancy, mimicking what Emma had said to her the previous term. 'Now, is Lucy going to show us this floor routine of hers or what?'

Lucy had always been particularly excellent on the floor: all her ballet training lent her dance elements a grace and fluidity that reminded Ellie of Casey Cottrell. She didn't have the daring and razzmatazz of Katya, or the strength and power of Nancy, but she had something else – something that made her simply beautiful to watch.

'She's looking good, isn't she?' said Fran, coming over to stand by Ellie. Fran had a gentle manner as a coach which was totally different to Oleg's ranting, Sasha's giddy excitement, or even Emma's sombre, serious ways. But she really cared about her gymnasts and knew how to get the best out of them.

'She's – wonderful!' said Ellie.

'How about you?' said Fran. 'I hear you've been working on a new piece with Casey. Are you pleased with how it's going?'

'Yeah – I mean, I think so,' said Ellie.

Fran looked at her quizzically. She'd coached Ellie since she was five years old and could tell when something wasn't quite right.

'It's just a bit more modern than the routines I've had before,' explained Ellie. 'More daring.'

'I suppose that makes sense,' said Fran. 'Lizzie was always a very flamboyant performer. I guess Casey thinks you might suit that style too.'

'But Lizzie was much more confident on the floor than I am, wasn't she?'

'What makes you say that?' said Fran with a

frown. 'Your aunt was more nervous about the floor than any other piece of apparatus. She said she hated feeling like she was in the spotlight.'

'Really?' Ellie looked at Fran in surprise. There were so many things she wanted to ask Fran about Lizzie. Had she heard from her lately? Did she know what she was up to now? Did she ever ask how Ellie was doing?

But there was no time for questions, because just then Tam came in to tell them that it had started snowing again. 'And we'll be late for your dad if we don't get a move on,' he added. 'I reckon he'll want to get going as soon as possible in case the weather gets worse.'

As they gathered all their things, pulling on thick coats and woolly hats over their tracksuits, Fran said to Ellie, 'Don't give up on that routine. You just need to find the daredevil performer inside yourself. And I know she's in there somewhere!'

Ellie hugged Fran tightly. 'Thanks,' she said. 'I hope you're right.'

CHAPTER
Eighteen

As they left the gym the snow was falling. 'It really feels like Christmas Eve, doesn't it!' said Nancy, as they made their way through the town, past shop windows full of tinsel and baubles and a choir singing carols in the snowy town marketplace.

'In Russia, we celebrate Christmas Eve,' said Katya who had really perked up after the gym session. She seemed to have forgotten her seasickness, for a bit at least. 'A big feast, and presents too.'

'Then maybe we should have a Russian Christmas tonight,' suggested Tam.

'And English Christmas tomorrow!' said Lucy

excitedly. 'That way we get to do it twice!'

'Sounds good to me,' said Nancy. 'But if this weather gets any worse we may not make it back for even one Christmas, let alone two – come on!'

Nancy was right. By the time they met Dad down at the harbour, the mist was starting to roll in from the sea. 'Best get a move on before it's impossible to see where we're going,' said Dad.

So they all clambered aboard *Diablo* again, with Katya declaring loudly that this was the last boat she was ever going on for the rest of her life.

'Tell you what, why don't we sing Christmas carols to take your mind off the water?' suggested Tam, seeing that Katya was looking genuinely scared. Underneath his joking exterior, he had a very warm heart.

So as *Diablo* made her way out of the harbour and past the headland towards open sea, the boat full of gymnasts sang as many Christmas tunes as they could think of. It didn't seem to matter that they could only remember the first verse of most of them – or that none of them could sing very well.

'You can see why we're gymnasts, not choristers!' Tam said after they'd squawked their way through 'Silent Night'. But it seemed to do the trick, making Katya giggle and taking her mind off the rolling waves underneath her.

The snow had started to fall more heavily and the white mist was getting thicker by the minute. Dad had switched on *Diablo*'s headlamp which cast a beam of yellow light out across the water in front of them, and they managed to make it along the coast – but as they turned into the mouth of the river estuary, the fog became so dense they could barely see more than ten metres in front of them.

'At least we're out of the open water,' said Dad who seemed incredibly calm. 'We'll have to go super slow from now on if we want to avoid hitting anything.'

'But the tide's going out, isn't it?' said Ellie. 'If we go too slow, aren't we in danger of missing the tide and getting stuck out on the mud flats?'

'We'll navigate a course along the centre of the estuary, where it's deepest,' said Dad. 'And I'll be keeping a close eye on the depth sounder.' He nodded at one of the instruments on the dashboard. 'It measures how deep the water is under the hull - so we can work out if we are getting close to grounding her. OK?'

Nancy nodded enthusiastically. She found anything to do with boats absolutely fascinating.

'Ellie, I'm going to turn off the engine and I want you and Nancy to help me row whilst I navigate,' said Dad. 'You'll find oars stowed under there. Do you think you can do it?'

'Of course we can,' said Nancy.

'Lucy, you keep an eye on Katya,' said Dad, glancing at Katya. She had gone pale as a ghost in the murky gloom and was shivering with cold and fear.

'What about me?' asked Tam.

Dad grinned. 'With your ability to capsize in the bath, it's probably best if you just keep singing.'

'His singing is nearly as dangerous as his rowing,' said Nancy, but Tam just pulled a face and launched into a loud and tuneless version of 'We Wish You a Merry Christmas.'

Moving much slower now with Nancy and Ellie on the oars and the engine turned off, *Diablo* navigated a course upriver. The mist was even thicker as it rolled off the snow-covered hillsides and filled the estuary with white air so dense that they could barely make out each other's faces in the gloom.

'What happens if we can't make it back?' said Tam, taking a break from his carolling to ask the question that was on everyone's mind.

'Well, we could moor up at the Ferryboat Inn,' said Dad. 'But we've got all the supplies for Christmas dinner on board.'

'Then we have to make it back, don't we?' said Lucy. 'We can't cancel Christmas!'

'We might have to if we get stuck out here on the mud flats,' said Nancy.

'At least we've got plenty of food on board,' Tam pointed out. 'We won't starve!'

'Always thinking of your stomach!' Nancy shook her head.

They were moving at a snail's pace now. Everything seemed eerily silent with just the splash of the oars rhythmically rising and falling and their breath coming in shallow puffs. It was incredibly hard work. *Diablo* was a far bigger vessel than either Ellie or Nancy was used to. Luckily, their gym training and Oleg's army-style conditioning regime meant that they both had strength and endurance, although Ellie found she was barely able to keep up with Nancy's powerful strokes.

It felt almost like a dream, rowing through the water, engulfed in a blanket of cloud. They could have been anywhere, Ellie thought. No familiar landmarks were visible. Their progress was slow and laborious and they were all conscious of the tide turning and the creek waters getting shallower and shallower by the minute.

'We've gone past the Ferryboat Inn,' said Nancy. 'I could make out the lights on their pontoon. We should be passing the sailing club round about now.'

'Then we'll be turning into the creek,' said Dad. 'This is the trickiest bit.'

Katya whimpered from the back of the boat. Lucy put her arm around her and held her close.

157

Ellie thought of Katya fearlessly walking along the washing line and flying through the air on a trapeze. She seemed almost like a different person now.

Everyone seemed to be holding their breath as Dad focused on the depth charger to navigate the boat down through the narrow channel of remaining water. Tam had even stopped singing. But Dad knew this stretch of water like the lines on his own hand. He'd grown up on the creek – his great grandfather had built Trengilly Cottage, and his grandfather had started the boat building business. This stretch of river was in his blood.

'Did you know that during the war, Ellie's great grandfather used to take British spies over to France in the middle of the night?' Dad asked, his voice sounding vaguely muffled in the mist. 'He had to go without engines, no visibility. Just like this.'

'Really?' said Ellie. She vaguely remembered Dad telling her about how he and Lizzie had played 'spies' out on the creek, but she had no idea it had been inspired by their grandfather's real-life heroics.

'He told me a story once,' Dad went on. 'He

and a young British officer missed the tide and got caught out on the mud flats by Frenchman's Creek.'

'What happened to them?' asked Ellie.

'They had to wait till the next high tide,' said Dad. The splash of the oars was the only sound in the mist other than his voice. 'It was deep winter, like this. They stayed out all night. Never been so cold in his life, my grandad said. But they made it back.'

'Wow!' said Tam.

'It was just before the D–Day landings,' Dad went on. 'Your granddad said the intelligence the officer bought was vital to the success of the mission.'

'Well, our mission is to deliver the turkey safely to Trengilly Cottage,' said Tam. 'And we will not fail!'

And he was right. Looming through the mist now they could just make out the murky shapes of the boatshed and the pontoon. And there were lights too, shining along the beach, lights that weren't usually there.

'It's Mum!' shouted Lucy.

'And Mandy too!' said Ellie, relief flooding

through her. She hadn't realised how frightened she'd actually been until that moment.

The two mums had strung out Christmas lights along the beach to guide the travellers home through the mist. As the boat crept closer they could see both women standing on the pontoon holding lanterns.

'Careful!' said Nancy. 'The depth sounder is reading just over a metre.'

'How much water do we need to get in?' Tam asked.

'About a metre,' said Dad. 'It's going to be close shave.'

Everyone held their breaths as Dad navigated the final stretch. As they neared the pontoon they could hear the mums shouting out greetings.

They were about ten metres away from the pontoon now and suddenly the depth sounder started beeping alarmingly. 'I reckon you all need to bundle out here,' said Dad. 'Get the supplies out so that the boat weighs a bit less, then I'll see if I can moor her.'

Ellie, Nancy and Lucy clambered out. It was a

shock wading out through the freezing water, even though it only came up as high as their knees.

'Hey, it's like one of Oleg's ice baths,' said Nancy, as they held the bags of shopping high over their heads and struggled over to the pontoon, where Mum and Mandy helped pull them up out of the water and enveloped them in hugs. Ellie could see the worry etched on their faces now – and that told her they had been in more trouble than Dad had ever let on.

But Katya was too terrified to get out of the boat. None of Dad's coaxing, or the girls' encouragement, could make her budge.

'I'll carry you,' said Tam, speaking softly, like she was a small child. 'Come on. Piggyback?'

Katya looked up at him uncertainly.

'I promise not to drop you,' he said gently. 'So long as you promise you won't kiss me any more! Is it a deal?'

'Deal!' stammered Katya, clambering on to his back and letting him carry her safely to shore. As he set her down on dry land, she immediately went to hug him.

'Uh–uh!' said Tam, backing off and shaking his head. 'Remember your promise!'

'OK,' said Katya. 'But you save my life so I love you for ever!'

'No saying stuff like that in front of Robbie,' Tam groaned. 'Or I might just throw you back in the creek!'

An hour later they'd all thawed out in front of the roaring fire and were drinking hot soup (nettle, chilli and garlic – one of Mum's surprisingly nice specials) and telling Mum and Mandy all about the day's adventures.

'Oleg will be thrilled when he hears we've been having ice baths in the frozen river,' said Ellie.

'Yeah, that's real dedication to his Romanian training regime,' grinned Tam.

At Lucy's suggestion they decided to have a Russian Christmas Eve after supper. They munched on mince pies and were each allowed one gift to open. Lucy's, from Mum and Dad, was a brand new pair of hand-guards in white leather with her initials embossed on them in gold.

'They'll be perfect when you come to the Academy,' said Ellie with a smile.

Tam got a cookbook from Nancy. 'You go on about food so much it's about time you learned to actually cook some!' she told him.

Ellie and Nancy had bought an old-fashioned snow globe for Katya. Inside the glass ball was a big top, a clown and a tightrope artist who magically seemed to dance across the high wire as the snow fell around her.

'Is perfect!' said Katya, smothering both girls with kisses. 'Reminds me of home!'

Mandy, Tam and Nancy had clubbed together to get Ellie an Academy tracksuit. 'Because you can't turn up to the British in your games kit!' said Nancy.

Ellie gazed at the beautiful tracksuit. It was in the Academy colours of blue and silver, with the squad logo on the breast and 'Academy Ellie' written on the back in sparkling silver letters. She loved that it didn't say 'Ellie Trengilly'. Nancy and Tam knew that she wanted to be recognised for her own achievements, not for the Trengilly name.

Nancy was last to receive her present.

'Wait a moment. We have to go and get it.' Ellie grinned at Lucy and they disappeared outside, returning a couple of minutes later with a gift that was long and very heavy – and wrapped in old sheets.

'Sorry! We couldn't find any wrapping paper big enough,' Ellie explained.

But Nancy didn't reply. As she pulled away the sheets to reveal a pair of sleek new handmade oars, she just gasped.

'She's actually speechless,' said Tam. 'This is a world first!'

'I – I . . . Oh, wow!' Nancy managed to whisper.

'Dad made them for you,' Lucy said. 'But it was Ellie's idea.'

'Do you like them?' asked Ellie, suddenly anxious because Nancy had tears flooding down her cheeks.

'I – I love them!' Nancy gulped. 'I've never had a more wonderful present in my life.'

Lucy beamed. 'Turn them over!'

Nancy did and there, written along the blade of

each, were the words 'Nancy Moffat'.

'Mum and I did that,' said Lucy proudly.

'So now you're a proper oarswoman, Nancy Moffat,' said Dad. 'And thank goodness you are, because if it weren't for you and Ellie we might still be stuck out on the mud flats tonight!'

CHAPTER
Nineteen

The Christmas holidays flew by all too quickly. Christmas Day was noisy and crazy and brilliant fun. Everyone squeezed around the kitchen table at Trengilly Cottage to tuck into a giant Christmas lunch of turkey and all the trimmings, followed by more present-opening and a riotous game of charades. On Boxing Day they went sledging up on Calamansac Hill and made snow gymnasts on the beach. Lucy's 'girl doing splits' was voted the best, whilst Tam's 'boy on the pommel horse' looked more like a dog with weird ears, according to Nancy – although her own attempt to do a gymnast on the bars collapsed into a giant heap before Mum came out to judge.

By New Year the roads were just about passable in Dad's Land Rover (the Academy minibus was still buried deep in a snowdrift) and so they spent New Year's Eve at the Sailing Club, where there were fireworks, a hog roast and a disco. They saw in the New Year sitting on the quay, watching the fireworks exploding high over the water. They all fell silent and Ellie wondered if they were making their wishes for the year to come. She suspected that hers, Katya's and Tam's were all the same: to do well at the British. And she could guess Lucy's too. Staring up at the dark bowl of the sky, the multi-coloured rain of stars reflected in her eyes, Ellie knew that Lucy was dreaming of getting into the Academy.

Then she glanced at Nancy. Her face was set in concentration as she stared out across the creek, but Ellie couldn't tell what she was thinking. What was Nancy wishing for? She looked – not sad exactly – more as if she was making up her mind about something. And at that moment Ellie changed her New Year's wish. Instead of asking for success for herself she fixed her eyes on a star and wished that Nancy's dreams might come true this year . . . whatever they were.

To celebrate New Year's Day, Mum had taken Lucy and Katya to watch the *Snow Queen* ballet which was showing at the theatre in town. Tam helped Dad collect lobster pots in the estuary, and Ellie and Nancy sat together on the pontoon, staring out at the creek. They'd just been out for a rowing session, but Ellie couldn't be persuaded to go for a swim in the icy water, despite Nancy's begging.

'I just can't wait to get back into the gym, can you?' Ellie asked, her feet dangling down off the pontoon, toes skimming the water. With Fran's gym having been closed over the New Year and the beach as hard as ice, Ellie was positively aching to start training again.

'Actually,' said Nancy, 'I'm not coming back.'

'What?' Ellie turned to her in surprise.

'I've been waiting for the right moment to tell you,' said Nancy. 'I've been talking to Mum – and your parents too – and I've made a decision.' She hesitated for a second before saying, 'I'm giving up gymnastics.'

'But – you're so talented,' Ellie stammered. 'So good.'

'Not quite good enough,' said Nancy, looking away with a shrug. 'To get to the top, a gymnast needs to be able to conquer her nerves. And I don't think I'm ever going to be able to do that.'

Ellie wanted to say something, but no words came. She'd known in her heart that this day might come but she still didn't want to believe it.

'Actually, I think I let go of the dream long ago,' Nancy went on. 'It just took coming back here to realise it.'

'You don't really mean that,' Ellie managed to say at last.

'I do.' Nancy looked up and smiled a little sadly. 'When I'm here, rowing – even on the night we thought we were going to get stuck out on the mud flats – I'm still ten times happier than I've been at the Academy recently.'

Ellie could feel tears welling in her eyes. She knew how unhappy Nancy had been, and she knew deep down that this was the right thing for her.

'So – if it's OK with you – I'm going to stay here,' Nancy said. 'With your mum and dad! It was your dad's idea. Mum wasn't sure at first, but she's seen how happy I am here and she's come round to it.'

'Of course it's OK! You're pretty much family anyway.'

'I'm thinking of it as trading places with you!' said Nancy. 'I get to live with your family and you get to live with mine. Your dad says I can join the local gig rowing team. He thinks there might be opportunities for me to work with a coach he knows who trained one of the Olympic rowing teams. And there are amazing sailing competitions too. It's my idea of heaven!'

'So basically, you're swapping one Olympic dream for another?' Ellie knew just how competitive Nancy could be when it came to rowing.

'Maybe,' said Nancy. 'For now I just need a break from the pressure. To remember what it feels like to do a sport for fun again, you know?'

Ellie looked at her friend and suddenly she understood. This was what Nancy had been wishing for at New Year. She was barely able to keep the tears from spilling out now.

'Tam reckons Head-Over-Heels House will be way more peaceful without me!' grinned Nancy.

'He doesn't mean that,' said Ellie with a loud sniff. 'He'll miss you more than anyone – well, anyone except me!'

'Oh, I'll be Skyping you every day,' said Nancy. 'And Mum's insisting I come home twice a month, to give your parents a break – though why they'd want a break from me, I can't imagine!'

Ellie made a sound that was half giggle, half sob. 'But still – oh, Nancy. I'm . . .' She barely knew what to say.

'I know,' said Nancy simply. 'I feel the same way.'

The snow had started to fall again, in slow meandering drifts. Ellie put her arms around her friend and pulled her tight.

'I figure we'll still go the Olympics together one day,' Nancy said. 'Only I'll be a Team GB rower, and you'll be on the gym squad.'

'And we'll both win golds,' sniffed Ellie.

'Lots of them,' said Nancy. 'We might even let Tam win one too, if he behaves himself!'

Ellie grinned and looked her friend right in the eye. 'And no matter what happens, we'll always be best friends.'

'Of course,' said Nancy. 'Forever!'

CHAPTER
Twenty

Two days later they all helped Dad dig the Academy minibus out of its snowdrift, then Tam, Katya, Mandy and Ellie drove back to London, leaving Nancy and the rest of the Trengilly family behind. Waving goodbye to the creek felt even harder than ever for Ellie: this time she was leaving her best friend behind too.

It felt so quiet in Head-Over-Heels House without Nancy when they arrived that evening that Ellie was glad she was still sharing a room with Katya. Her crazy chatter helped take Ellie's mind off the sight of the empty top bunk.

The next day though, at training, there was nothing to stop Ellie feeling Nancy's absence. Oleg was fiercer than ever, declaring that the holiday had turned them all soft.

'One week out of the gym and you need four weeks to get back to level!' he barked, as he made the girls do endless shuttle runs, plank walks, and excruciating stretches.

Ellie knew Nancy would have had something silly to say to take her mind off the pain. Without her, the session was agony.

'Junior British Championships are only six weeks away,' Oleg went on. 'You must all work harder than you ever work before, or you not be ready.'

He was tougher than ever on mistakes, too. Ellie's preparation for the Challenge Cup meant she was looking good on everything except the floor – but there he was constantly picking her up on tiny errors. He never seemed satisfied. 'No! No! No!' he would bark, stamping his tiny little foot angrily. 'Not like this! Not like you are going to funeral!' He pulled a sad face so exaggerated it would have been funny if Ellie hadn't been feeling so despondent. 'Do you want to kill judges with boredom?'

Ellie shook her head, fought back the sudden desire to cry, and tried again, focusing on every tiny detail Oleg had picked out. She was determined to land every tumble, ace every leap and spin every turn flawlessly. But any magic dust she'd picked up in the circus seemed to have rubbed off long ago. In fact, since Nancy had left, Ellie was sure she was getting worse rather than better. Oleg seemed to think the same. 'You perform daring routine, you need to do it brilliantly,' he told her. 'You must sparkle, then even judges who hate it will have no choice but to love it!'

This didn't exactly help. Being told the judges might hate the routine only made her more anxious to get it right, and that seemed to lead to more mistakes, until by the end of the session Ellie was usually close to tears. She had never felt less sparkly in her life.

At least all the other gymnasts were all being extra nice to Ellie - except Scarlett, of course. She took

175

every opportunity to point out how much quieter things were without Nancy.

'At least *she* had the sense to realise that she was never going to make it,' she said, glancing pointedly at Katya, as the girls from each squad got changed together. 'Some people just never get the hint.'

Nancy had once said that Scarlett was only nice to you as long as she didn't think you were a threat. Now that Ellie and Katya had qualified for the British, it seemed like they were back on Scarlett's hit list.

'I guess we'll see who can deliver at Junior British Champs,' said Kashvi, rolling her eyes behind Scarlett's back. 'Won't we?'

'And so will the GB coaches,' added Bella. 'Remember, Barbara Steele and the other selectors will be there looking to pick girls for the Junior National Team.'

Ellie remembered what her sister had said about extra funding for GB squad members but earning a place was beginning to seem impossible.

'Well, first-timers or people who can't even

do a basic bar routine will hardly appear in the top ten,' said Scarlett. Ellie flushed. She couldn't help wishing Nancy were here to give a quick put down. Luckily Katya didn't seem to be offended. 'Is true,' she declared cheerfully. 'The bars, always my enemy!'

'But the selectors don't just look at the top ten,' said Bella. 'They also look at girls who excel on particular pieces of apparatus.'

'Which means that if Ellie can ace it on the bars, or Katya wows with her beam, they'll be in with a chance. And we all know they're incredible on those pieces!' added Kashvi loyally. 'They could make it, top ten or not!'

Scarlett scowled. 'Well, the Academy's got a reputation to uphold. I just hope the rest of us aren't made to look bad. The competition from other clubs will be fierce.'

'Then we'll just have to show them that the Academy girls are even better!' said Kashvi. 'Won't we!'

*

177

For the next few days, Ellie tried to share the other girls' excitement about the British, but still nothing was going right. She couldn't shake off her anxiety about her floor routine, and without Nancy to joke and chat with in training everything seemed flat.

Before long, Ellie found she was longing to go back to circus school. Maybe she could pick up another sprinkling of magic dust and remind herself how to have fun with gymnastics. Katya also seemed to be pining for the big top. Ellie reckoned she needed the circus like a normal person needed oxygen – she couldn't survive without it.

They'd made a plan to go at the weekend, and this time Tam had agreed to come too – but on Sunday morning, when Ellie went to find him, she found him hanging out with Robbie in the kitchen at Head-over-Heels House. Robbie was munching on one of Mandy's cupcakes, and he grinned broadly when he saw Ellie and jabbed Tam in the ribs.

'Here comes your lady friend,' he said.

Ellie ignored him. 'Um, we're off to Covent Garden,' she said, using the code they'd agreed on for circus school. 'You ready, Tam?'

Robbie smirked. 'Ooh! *are* you ready, Tam?' he asked, a stupid grin plastered over his face.

Tam glanced at Robbie, then back to Ellie, and his jaw tightened. 'Actually, I'm kind of busy,' he said. 'You guys go without me.'

'Oh, right,' said Ellie, flushing slightly. 'Only, I thought . . .'

Robbie was looking from one to the other, still smirking.

'Maybe another time,' said Tam, quickly.

'Fine – um – OK then.' Ellie turned away, feeling disappointed and confused. She'd been looking forward to spending the day with Tam, who was the closest thing she had to Nancy these days. She couldn't understand why he was suddenly being so weird.

She was still puzzling it over when she and Katya bumped into Scarlett on the way out.

'Going *nowhere* again?' Scarlett asked, looking suspiciously at their tracksuits and catching the guilty flush that immediately rushed to Ellie's cheeks.

'Covent Garden, actually,' said Ellie quickly. 'I'm showing Katya the sights.'

'Really?' Scarlett raised a single eyebrow. 'Well, have fun!' she said super-cheerfully. 'Don't forget to tell us all about it when you get back.'

'Um – yeah,' said Ellie hastily. 'We will.'

Scarlett's friendliness made Ellie nervous, but she pushed it out of her mind as she and Katya made their way over to circus school. After a week of Oleg's gruelling back-to-the-gym regime – and with no Nancy to help her laugh her way through it – she figured he deserved a bit of circus fun!

That afternoon, Dee Dee showed them how to use the trapeze, something Ellie had been longing to try ever since she had seen Katya flying through the air on their very first visit to Circus Pocus. Ellie absolutely loved being airborne – it reminded her of the bars, which had always been her favourite piece of apparatus – but it was also different, requiring greater bendiness and less rigidity than she was used to.

'I still don't really get how you can be so good at

this but find bars so tricky,' said Ellie, after Katya had taught her a thrilling catch-and-release manouevre which required her to fling herself from one trapeze to the other. She'd just fallen into the netting for the fifth time in a row, and she was gladder than ever that she had a safety harness on.

'I too am not able to explain this,' said Katya with a shrug.

'Tell you what, why don't you teach me how you do the trapeze,' said Ellie. 'And then maybe I can help figure out what's going wrong with your bars.'

So they spent the afternoon airborne, and Katya proved to be a very good teacher. She helped Ellie to let go of her inhibitions and learn new tricks, even making her laugh at the same time. Ellie quickly started to get the hang of it, and it felt amazing. Up in the air, she could almost imagine she was in the circus, a showgirl decked out in sequins and feathers, dazzling the packed big top as she spun and sparkled through the spotlight. The sensation was intoxicating. If only she could feel like this when she performed on the floor! But for now it was just enough to be able to let go and forget her worries for a while.

In fact, they had so much fun that when they arrived back at Head-Over-Heels House, just in time for supper, Ellie realised that she hadn't thought about Nancy all afternoon.

Tam wasn't around, but the rest of their housemates were sitting round the giant dining table enjoying a supper of goulash. 'Cooked in honour of my favourite little Russian gymnast!' Mandy smiled at Katya as the girls tucked in hungrily.

'So, how was Covent Garden?' asked Scarlett, looking up from her food with a friendly smile on her face.

'Oh, was wonderful!' said Katya. 'I like to see so many beautiful flowers.'

Scarlett lifted a forkful of goulash and studied it as if it was the most interesting thing in the world. 'Um – you do realise that Covent Garden isn't actually a garden, right?' she said, not altering her super-sweet tone.

Katya went pink, and Ellie's heart seemed to do a backflip.

Scarlett swallowed her mouthful of goulash and licked her lips as Ellie struggled desperately to think what to say.

'Yeah, but it used to be a flower market,' said a voice from behind her. Ellie turned round to see Tam, standing in the doorway with Robbie at his side. She didn't think she'd ever been so glad to see him. 'I thought everyone knew that.'

It was Scarlett's turn to flush now and Ellie tried to give Tam a grateful smile but he just went to sit on the other side of the table with Robbie.

'I say something wrong?' whispered Katya, glancing over to where Scarlett was still watching them suspiciously. 'I thinking garden means grass and trees and flowers. Is not right?'

'No – it was my fault,' whispered Ellie, her heart still hammering in her chest. 'I should have told you that it was a different kind of garden.'

'Tam is saving me again!' grinned Katya.

'Yup, I think he just saved us both' agreed Ellie.

She tried to catch Tam's eye again, but he was laughing at some joke with Robbie and didn't seem to notice. And when she tried to go and thank him after supper, he'd disappeared again. Mandy said that he and Robbie were working on a homework project in his room. Ellie couldn't help but feel a twinge of disappointment. She and the twins had always done homework together in the past.

'Oh, don't mind him,' said Nancy when Ellie Skyped Trengilly Cottage that evening to fill them in on the afternoon's near miss with Scarlett. 'He's probably just bonding with the boys' squad.'

'I guess,' said Ellie. 'And I suppose now you're gone, he probably doesn't want to hang out with a load of girls anyway.'

'His loss!' shrugged Nancy, grinning.

'Tell us more about Scarlett!' said Lucy, who was huddled next to Nancy at the kitchen table in Trengilly Cottage. 'Do you think she's sussed you out?'

'She is like detective!' said Katya.

'You have to put her off the scent,' said Nancy.

'If she finds out, she'll totally rat on you and then you'll be banned from going – and worse!'

'I know,' said Ellie.

'But if I not go to circus I think I will pop!' said Katya.

'And you can't let Katya Popolova go pop!' said Lucy.

The others all giggled, but Ellie barely managed a smile. Scarlett's snooping had reminded her of all she had to lose if they were caught. She shivered. It was too awful to think about. But she couldn't bear to give up the circus now, any more than Katya could. If she could just bottle a bit of the magic she had felt up on the trapeze and put it into her performance on floor, then maybe – just maybe – she could be noticed by the Team GB selectors. So she was willing to take the risk. They'd just have to be more careful from now on.

CHAPTER
Twenty-One

'Would it be OK if – I mean – can Katya and I stay late this week?' Ellie asked Sasha at the end of training the next day. 'I said I'd help her with that bar skill she's struggling with. That is, if you don't mind.'

After having Scarlett snooping around last week, Ellie and Katya had decided it would be safer for a while to concentrate on their skills in the gym – especially working on Katya's bar routine.

'Fine,' said Sasha with a smile. 'Sian's working late most nights this week. You and Katya can have an extra half an hour. If you can help her, then that's great.'

'Thanks,' said Ellie.

It was nice having the gym virtually to themselves. Sian Edwards was working on an insanely difficult Produnova vault that she was hoping to perform at European Championships later in the year, but otherwise the gym was deserted. And Ellie found she enjoyed being a coach. Working with Katya on the trapeze, Ellie had spotted a few ways to help her on the bars. It was a challenge trying to get Katya to translate her circus skills into a more successful bar routine, but she was quick and keen to learn. By the end of the first session, she was still far from perfect, but she was starting to get it. All the same, she was not happy.

'I still not understand why so many rules!' moaned Katya as they got changed afterwards. 'Straight back, legs together, no arching, no pausing, no stepping back on landing ... In circus is all about performance!'

'Did you ever think that execution and performance might be the same thing?' asked a voice from the doorway.

Ellie looked up to see Sian Edwards. She had

finished training and had come to collect her stuff.

'I no understand,' said Katya.

'Think about it,' said Sian, pulling an old pair of leggings and a T-shirt out of her gym bag and tugging them on. 'Clear lines, unbroken rhythms – they make a routine more beautiful to watch.'

'I suppose so,' Katya sighed. 'Sometimes I think gymnastics is most confusing sport in world!'

'That's because it's more than a sport,' said Sian, zipping up her gym bag, and walking to the door. 'It's also an art form. And if you want to succeed, you need to make it both.'

Ellie watched Sian leave. She felt her eyes shining with newly ignited ambition. What Sian had said felt so right. It wasn't *either* rules *or* performance – you had to do both if you wanted to make it to the top. And as the door closed behind Sian, Ellie realised she wanted that more than anything else in the whole world.

January seemed to go by in a blur. What with extra-long training sessions, helping Katya in the gym after hours, loads of tests at school and the short winter days, Ellie felt as if she barely did anything other than eat, sleep, go to school and go to the gym.

But as the weeks went on, she still couldn't seem to adjust to Nancy not being around. Even though she chatted to her and Lucy almost every night, it wasn't the same. And she was missing Tam too. She hardly seemed to see him at all any more. In fact, sometimes she had the feeling he was deliberately avoiding her. Ellie started to wonder if Nancy had been the glue that had held them together. Now she was gone, there was nothing to keep them friends. Or perhaps Tam had never really been Ellie's friend at all.

Ellie was surprised how much this idea upset her, so she was glad when Katya insisted Tam come along to circus school with them the next Sunday.

He'd initially said no – but then Robbie had announced he was going to his grandparents' for the day and Tam had changed his mind.

'None of the other lads are around, so I figure I might as well hang with you', he said at breakfast.

189

Katya was jumping up and down excitedly. 'Goody!' she squeaked, forgetting to whisper. 'Is special clown day today – Harry will be teaching us to be silly!'

'Where are you off to?' asked Scarlett. Ellie turned round and saw her in the doorway. She wondered how long she'd been standing there. 'Did I hear you mention clowns?'

'Yeah, there's a special circus exhibition at the V&A museum,' said Tam, without even a moment's hesitation. 'We thought Katya would enjoy it.'

'Sounds fun,' said Scarlett, sitting down and tucking into a massive bowl of porridge smothered with honey and strawberries. 'I'll have to check it out sometime.'

'Cool,' said Tam, winking at Katya. 'Anyway, we've gotta dash. These museums won't be there forever, you know!'

'Was that true?' Ellie asked later, as they headed off to Circus Pocus. 'Is there really a circus exhibition?'

'No,' laughed Tam. 'But she put me on the spot. I had to think of something.'

'You had me convinced,' said Ellie, smiling. 'Let's just hope she doesn't decide to go on a gallery visit!'

Any awkwardness between Tam and Ellie seemed to melt as they made their way across the park towards circus school. Even the weather seemed to have improved, making Ellie feel happier than she had since Nancy left. There were snowdrops and crocuses budding around the trees, and when they arrived at Circus Pocus they found shafts of sunlight streaming through the giant warehouse windows, casting a golden glow over everything.

'Hey there!' said Harry when he saw Tam. 'Who's this?'

'Our friend, Tam. He is gymnast too,' said Katya. 'Working very hard for British!'

'Yeah, well, boys have six pieces of apparatus to master so there's no time for messing around,' said Tam with a grin. 'Not like the lazy girls who only have to do four!'

Ellie knew that if Nancy had been there she'd have made some quick retort – or just punched her brother. All she could think to do was roll her eyes.

'The girls don't have much time for fun either, by the sounds of it,' said Dee Dee. Today she had dyed her crazy hair pink and purple, and was wearing a clown hat perched on top of it.

'Well, you've come to the right place,' said Harry. 'In the big top you can blow all your cares away. You gonna enrol in clown school for the afternoon?'

'I'm not sure clowning is for me,' said Ellie, glancing nervously at the giant pairs of shoes lined up in the ring and the group of kids wearing clown noses.

'Uh-uh! There's no way are you getting out of this, Miss Trengilly!' said Tam, grabbing her by the arm and dragging her over to the ring. 'Come on.'

So that afternoon, Ellie and Katya and Tam put on giant shoes, red noses, funny hats and big gloves, and Harry taught them the art of clowning. Although Ellie struggled a bit more than Tam and Katya with the really silly stuff, it was much more fun than she'd expected. It was more acrobatic, too – and totally exhausting.

After the little kids had gone, Harry asked Tam

and the girls if they wanted to help him with a new act he was working on.

'It's for a touring show that Dee Dee and me are gonna be appearing in,' he explained.

'So, how can we help?' asked Tam.

Harry was going to ride a giant ten foot high unicycle whilst balancing plates and cups on a long stick. The aim was to pile them up as high as possible, then put a cup and saucer on the very top and pour a cup of tea – all while he kept cycling. It seemed crazy and impossible to Ellie, but it would be great if he could pull it off.

'You throw the plates,' said Harry. 'An' I'm gonna catch 'em!'

'That sounds easy enough,' said Ellie.

'No fun to watch if it's too easy,' said Harry. 'That's why you've gotta throw them while you're tumbling!'

'Wait, so we throw the plates whilst we somersault?' asked Tam.

'Eggs-act-ly!' said Harry with a big grin. 'Gotta have good aim, or I'm never gonna catch 'em.'

'And you need to sell it too,' said Dee Dee with a smile.

'What do you mean "sell it"?' asked Ellie.

'Like this,' said Dee Dee. She took a plate off Harry, leapt into the ring and immediately seemed to switch into performance mode. She held the plate in the air and showed it off to an imaginary audience before inviting them to guess what she was going to do, beckoning them into the act with her eyes and her smile. 'Can I do it?' she seemed to be asking them. 'Do you want me to try?'

Then she went into a tumble, plate grasped between her teeth, landing in tuck-back and sending the plate spinning up into the air at the same time. It flew up, and for a second Ellie thought she'd missed – but Harry sprung forwards and caught the plate just in the nick of time. Dee Dee curtsied as Tam, Ellie and Katya burst into applause.

'See? You gotta big the whole thing up,' said Dee Dee as she came to join them. 'Tell a story!'

'How did you do that without saying a word?' asked Tam.

'That is the art of performance, my boy!' said Harry.

They spent the next hour helping Harry with his new act. Ellie enjoyed pretending to be Dee Dee, teasing the imaginary audience, although she was less successful at getting the plates on target.

'Thank goodness they're plastic plates,' said Tam, as the three of them made their way home through the park later.

'Otherwise we are like cows in a china shop!' said Katya, who was walking between the two of them, her arms tucked into theirs.

'Or even bulls in a china shop?' suggested Tam with a grin.

'That is what I say!' said Katya. 'My English is getting better – yes?'

'Your English is perfect!' said Ellie.

'If it gets any better it'll be boring!' added Tam, winking at Ellie. She grinned back. It was great to have Tam around again.

CHAPTER
Twenty-Two

Scarlett didn't quiz them about their day out when they got back. In fact, she wasn't even around at supper – her godmother was in town and had taken her out to a posh restaurant. So it looked like their circus secret was still safe.

But as soon as Ellie walked into the gym the next morning, she knew something was up. She and Katya were early, so only a few other gymnasts had arrived, but there, standing in the middle of the blue floor waiting for them, was Oleg. He had his arms crossed and was tutting angrily. At his side stood Scarlett, wearing a new sea-green leotard and looking very pleased with herself.

'Is this true?' demanded Oleg, his red face clashing comically with the purple and yellow tracksuit he was wearing. 'What I am hearing – about my gymnasts risking injuries – breaking Academy rules, sneaking around? Is it true?'

Ellie felt herself flushing and heard Katya give a barely audible squeak. Scarlett was staring at them both with a smug expression on her face.

The rest of the gymnasts were starting to come into the gym now, and they looked on curiously as Oleg continued to bark. 'In Romania, gymnasts who break rules are expelled,' he said, tugging hard on his own ears as he yelled.' Out on their ears! On their ears I say!'

Ellie's heart was hammering in her chest – she knew exactly what he was going to say next.

'Look at this!' said Oleg, waving something in the air. A small, brightly-coloured flyer with a picture of a big top, and a clown's face. Ellie's heart seemed to stop beating entirely for a moment.

'So can you tell me it is not true?' demanded

SOMERSAULTS AND DREAMS

Oleg. 'That my gymnasts have not been risking their careers for a bit of fun in the circus? Can you?'

Ellie opened her mouth but no words came out. She could not have denied it anyway.

Scarlett smiled triumphantly. 'I knew it!' she said. 'I knew you were up to something!'

'How you find out?' Katya asked, close to tears.

'I picked up Ellie's coat by mistake and found the flyer in your pocket,' said Scarlett with a shrug.

'By mistake!' said Katya, incredulously. 'I not believe it. I think you snooping like a thief!'

'It not matter where she find it,' barked Oleg. 'What matter is you are not having permission to go to this circus.'

'But they did have permission!' said a chirpy voice from the other side of the gym. Ellie glanced up to see Sasha sauntering over, wearing a pale pink velvet tracksuit and a pearly smile. 'Coach Petrescu, I was fully aware that these gymnasts were attending Circus Pocus sessions.'

Ellie wondered for a moment if she was dreaming.

'In fact,' Sasha went on. 'I myself gave them permission to go.'

Scarlett's face fell. Oleg spluttered in confusion. 'You knew?' He sounded as astonished as Ellie felt.

'Of course. The circus is like one big family, isn't that right, cupcake?' Sasha grinned cheerfully at Katya, whose big violet eyes looked like they were going to pop out of her head. 'My friend Harry told me they'd expressed an interest in attending some sessions, and I thought they might each benefit from them.'

'But the risks!' spluttered Oleg. 'They could have been injured . . . it is not safe!'

'Don't be silly, Oleg my little muffin!' said Sasha, patting his arm affectionately. 'I trust Harry and Dee Dee as much as any coach at the Academy.'

Oleg looked nonplussed, and Ellie felt equally confused. Scarlett just seemed livid. 'Why were they sneaking around if they knew they had permission to go?' she demanded.

Sasha surveyed Scarlett coolly from beneath her false eyelashes. 'I asked them to keep it to themselves,' she replied. 'Not that it is your place to question coaches' decisions, Miss Atkins.'

Some of the other gymnasts giggled. Scarlett went pale.

'Or to come tale-telling and tittle-tattling!' added Oleg, crossly shoving the leaflet in Scarlett's direction. 'Interrupting Oleg's training schedule with gossip and rumour!'

'I'm sorry,' stammered Scarlett. 'I thought . . .'

'No thinking!' barked Oleg. 'To work – all of you – double time!'

Ellie barely had time to process what had just happened. Oleg launched into the most gruelling conditioning sequence, *ever*, and he didn't give the squad a moment's let-up for the whole training session. And today Sasha insisted that the Development squad work in complete silence too. It wasn't until they'd finished and Ellie made her way over to the changing room, muscles she hadn't even known she had aching, that she heard Sasha say, 'Ellie, Katya – can you stay back for a quick chat, please?'

Ellie's stomach dropped.

The coach was sitting on the high beam, her pink legs swinging to and fro as the two girls came to stand in front of her.

'So,' she said, surveying them from her perch with a twinkle in her eye. 'What exactly have you got to say for yourselves?'

'Did you know all along?' squeaked Katya.

'Of course I did,' said Sasha, calmly. 'Just as you both knew you were breaking the rules by not asking permission from the Academy.'

'But we could not ask you,' protested Katya. 'You would only say no!'

'Would I?' Sitting on the beam, Sasha towered over both girls. They had to look up at her as she went on, 'I actually thought it was rather a good idea when I heard.'

'Really?' said Ellie.

'Katya's been much more focused in training since she's been able to let off steam in the circus,' Sasha went on. 'And I had a feeling that you might learn something that no amount of training could

201

teach you, Ellie. We shall see if I was right.'

'Why you not say you knowing?' asked Katya, looking confused.

'Well, I figured the best punishment for lying was having to keep up the lie,' said Sasha, her face more serious now. 'Living with the fear of discovery was punishment enough in itself.'

Ellie had to admit that she was right. She had hated lying to the Academy, and having it all out in the open was almost a relief. Almost. But what was going to happen now?

'Are you – that is –' Ellie struggled to get the words out. 'Are you going to tell Emma?'

'She already knows,' said Sasha, jumping down from the beam cheerfully.

Ellie's heart sank. That was it then. She'd blown it.

'Strangely enough, she seems to be under the impression that you asked me for permission and I said yes,' added Sasha with a wink. 'But otherwise, she's fully up to speed.'

'I – I don't . . .' It took a moment for Ellie to take this in.

'You tell lie for us?' asked Katya, in astonishment. 'So we not get in trouble?'

'I know you think I hate you, Miss Popolova,' said Sasha, her eyes twinkling beneath her sparkly pink eyeshadow. 'But I'm not actually a complete monster, you know.'

'No, I not think that . . .' Katya started to say.

Sasha just raised a perfectly plucked eyebrow and went on: 'You and I have more in common than you think. Neither of us likes to play by the rules *all* the time!'

Katya looked as if she might faint with astonishment.

'I also happen to think that the circus and gymnastics complement each other rather well,' Sasha went on. 'In fact, I have a gift I've been meaning to give you.'

'For me?' stammered Katya. She seemed as though she might burst with astonishment at all the day's revelations. 'A present? What is?'

'Watch and see, cupcake!'

Sasha smiled mysteriously and made her way

over to the sound system. She inserted a CD, then stepped on to the gym floor.

The gym seemed strangely silent and empty now that all the other gymnasts had left. As Sasha struck a pose, Ellie felt a shiver of anticipation go down her spine. The day just kept getting weirder and weirder.

'What she doing?' whispered Katya.

'I think,' Ellie whispered, 'she's showing you your new floor routine.'

The music started and Sasha began to move. Ellie knew Sasha had been an incredible gymnast in her time, competing for the national team and performing in acrobatics shows around the world, but few of the gymnasts at the Academy had ever watched Sasha perform. Watching her now, it was clear how talented she had been – and that she hadn't lost any of it.

For Katya it must have felt like looking in a mirror. The routine seemed to catch Katya's personality perfectly: funny, crazy, determined, affectionate, but also full of longing for home, frightened sometimes, and at other times fearless. The routine had circus elements but it was more than that – it was also beautiful and poetic, funny and fabulous, hilarious and heartbreaking in turn.

When it finished Ellie burst into applause, but Katya said nothing. Her eyes were bright with moisture. Sasha walked over to where the girls were standing. She was breathless and smiling. 'You like it?'

'It's . . . brilliant!' said Ellie.

'And you?' Sasha looked at Katya now.

She gave a little gulp and then the words came out in a rush. 'I love it!' she said. 'Is it . . . is it for me?'

'Who else?' laughed Sasha. 'So, do you reckon we can call off hostilities and be friends now, Miss Popolova?'

Katya coloured. 'I sorry – I not mean . . .'

But Sasha was smiling and waving a dismissive hand. 'Hey, we're too alike, you and I, pumpkin,' she said. 'Both a pair of stubborn showgirls. Why don't we call a truce? Shake hands and be friends.'

Katya solemnly offered her hand to Sasha, who took it and shook it firmly.

'Good, now let's get working!' she said, switching back into coaching mode. 'Because you and I only have two weeks to get this routine ready for the British!'

CHAPTER
Twenty-Three

'I can't believe she knew all along!' exclaimed Nancy when Ellie told her what had happened.

'Yeah, and we also found out that it was Sasha who sent Toni to check Katya out at Popolov Circus,' said Ellie.

'She must be hearing on circus grapevine that I am good gymnast,' said Katya. 'Is thanks to her that I come to Academy.'

'And it's also thanks to her that neither of us got kicked out,' said Ellie. 'If she'd blown our cover we'd have been in deep, deep trouble!'

'I just wish I'd been there when Sasha gave

Scarlett that putdown!' sighed Nancy.

'Oh, you'd have loved to see her face,' grinned Ellie. 'Anyway, what's going on with you?'

'Well, I've got my first gig race coming up,' said Nancy. 'Can you believe I'm racing with Charlie Eke and Joe Bruton? Remember – the boys I beat in the regatta last year?'

'How could I forget?' laughed Ellie.

'Ooh – and Mum's got us tickets for British Champs!' said Lucy. 'We're coming to watch you!'

'Whoa! That is the best news ever!' said Ellie. She'd thought it would be too expensive and hadn't dared allow herself to even hope they might come.

'Well, we couldn't miss your first British, could we?' said Lucy. 'And Mum sold three paintings to an American tourist last week! We can't wait to see you!'

'Especially now you're famous,' said Nancy, waving a magazine around in front of the screen. 'Did you see the article about you in *Gymnast* magazine this week?'

'It's about you and Katya,' Lucy explained. 'The

girls who've come through the Challenge Cup to get to the Junior British.'

'They're calling you the "dark horses",' said Nancy. 'Listen.' She picked up the magazine and read out a sentence: '*The top flight of Junior gymnasts had better watch out, because hot on their heels arc u pair of newcomers set to challenge them in the medals tables.*'

Ellie felt suddenly dizzy, but Katya gave an excited little squeak.

'*Katya Popolova is a Russian sensation, plucked from the circus in Moscow,*' Nancy went on. '*She scored the highest beam result ever recorded at the Challenge Cup, so although she may struggle on other pieces of apparatus, we're certain to see Katya contending for medals in the beam finals.*'

'I am liking this,' said Katya happily. 'I am Russian sensation!' She did a little skip and then said, 'What it say about Ellie?'

'Listen to this,' said Lucy, snatching the magazine from Nancy and reading on: '*Ellie Trengilly's name will ring bells with all gymnastics fans. The niece of the famous Lizzie Trengilly, Ellie is an incredible bar worker.*

If she can find her personality on the floor, she could challenge her aunt's position as one of the greatest GB gymnasts of all time.'

'There's pictures of you too, look!' said Nancy, holding up the magazine to show a picture of Ellie on the bar and Katya doing the splits on the floor, a cheeky grin on her face that reminded Ellie of Harry the clown.

'This is just the kind of press that will make sure the Team GB selectors are watching you at the British,' said Lucy.

'Yup,' Nancy agreed. 'Barbara Steele will definitely have an eye on you now.'

Katya gave another little skip, but Ellie wasn't sure how to feel. She was uncomfortable being the centre of attention and the magazine article made her cringe – but getting into Team GB was her aim, and if this helped her get noticed that had to be good thing.

'Oh, tell Tam he got a mention too,' said Nancy. 'He's a hot favourite to make the Masters final.'

'And he's *Gymnast* magazine's "Hunk of the Week",' giggled Lucy. 'Look!'

She held up a page with a photo of Tam surrounded by love hearts and the slogan 'Gym Hunk'. Nancy fell about laughing.

'What is this word, "hunk"?' asked Katya, staring at the picture in bemusement. 'It sound like he a monster!'

'It means he's good looking – apparently,' said Nancy, rolling her eyes. 'Seriously, the readers of this magazine must need their eyes testing.'

'Your brother is nicest boy in world,' said Katya, who had considered Tam a hero ever since he had saved her from the waves on that fateful Christmas Eve voyage.

'Yeah, well, you can't tell him about this!' said Nancy. 'We don't want it going to his head, do we?!'

Ellie didn't need to worry about accidentally giving away the secret to Tam. For the next fortnight she barely got to see him, let alone talk to him. Everything was so busy in the lead up to the British and the gymnasts seemed to spend almost every waking hour at the Academy. And when they weren't training, Tam seemed to have gone back to avoiding her again.

Ellie was almost too busy to feel upset about it. She had so much else on her mind. There was so much riding on this competition, not just her future at the Academy but maybe Lucy's too. She could not afford to mess up.

It wasn't until the Academy gymnasts were getting on the minibus to go to Liverpool that Ellie bumped into Tam – literally! She came bowling round the corner with her suitcase and nearly crashed into him and Robbie.

'Oh, sorry,' she gasped. 'Didn't see you there.'

Robbie sniggered and Tam's jaw stiffened.

'You all set for the big competition?' he asked, not really looking her in the eye.

'Yeah – um – I hope so,' she said. He was being so weird that it made her feel awkward too. 'What about you?'

'Yeah, me too,' he said.

Neither of them seemed to know what to say for a moment. Some of the other boys appeared and

Robbie started telling a funny story about their coach. Ellie started to turn away, but then Tam stopped her.

'I've been meaning to tell you,' he said quietly. 'I went over to Circus Pocus last week.'

'Oh,' said Ellie, wondering why he hadn't invited her to come. It wasn't like they even had to tiptoe around any more now the circus was no longer a secret.

'You were training with Katya,' he said, perhaps reading the hurt expression on her face. 'Which is really nice of you, by the way. She tells me you're a great coach.'

'Right, thanks,' said Ellie. So Tam was still finding time to talk to Katya. It was just *her* he was ignoring.

'Anyway, Harry told me something,' Tam went on. 'About your Aunt Lizzie. I should have told you but . . .' He tailed off.

Ellie frowned. 'So what was it?'

'One of Harry's circus friends met Lizzie in America recently,' said Tam. 'She's coaching at one of the big gyms in California.'

'I don't understand,' said Ellie. Lizzie had vowed to give up gymnastics for good, but now she was working as a coach.

'I know,' Tam shrugged. 'Weird, right?'

Katya appeared, pulling a giant suitcase that was nearly as big as she was. Lexi and a few of the other girls were with her,

'Tam, man!' said Robbie. 'Stop flirting with the ladies and come and sit up back with the real gymnasts!'

'Hey!' said Katya. 'Girl gymnasts are way better than you silly boys!'

'Yeah, right!' laughed Robbie.

'Why don't we put it to ze test?' asked Camille, putting her hands on her hips and surveying Robbie coolly. 'See who gets on better at ze British, huh!'

'Yeah – Academy boys versus Academy girls!' said Kashvi with a grin.

'You're on!' said Robbie. 'Come on, Tam. No chatting with the opposition.'

'I'm sorry, I . . .' Tam rolled his eyes at Ellie and smiled apologetically as Robbie pulled him away.

Just for a second, things had felt normal between them again, but now the moment was over. 'I gotta go,' he said. 'We'll talk soon, right?'

'Right,' said Ellie.

'Oh, and one more thing.' Tam turned around, managing to shake Robbie off for a second. 'Casey is going to be at the British too. So you can ask her about Lizzie, yeah?'

He grinned again as he was bundled to the back of the minibus and Ellie tried to smile back. Suddenly, though, she didn't feel much like smiling. If Lizzie was coaching a rival team, she wasn't even sure she wanted to know about it. She'd dreamed of making it on to the national team and representing her country, just as her aunt had done. But now that dream seemed tainted. Because it wasn't just that Lizzie wasn't bothered about Ellie's gym career. She was coaching the opposition.

The bus journey up to Liverpool took several hours and they didn't arrive at the hotel until the evening. Even though Ellie had very little appetite, Oleg

215

insisted that they all ate huge bowls full of pasta and chicken and vegetables for dinner. Then, almost straight after, Emma ordered then all up to bed for an early night.

Ellie was sharing a room with Katya. She had been super excited, bouncing around on the beds, singing the music to her floor routine and performing bits of her beam whilst she was brushing her teeth. But despite her giddiness she seemed to get to sleep right away. Ellie lay awake for ages, thinking about competing in the big arena, about Barbara Steele and the GB selectors watching her, and what Tam had said about Aunt Lizzie.

She glanced over at Katya, who was now sprawled out on her back, smiling in her sleep. She reminded herself that none of Katya's family had been able to make it over to the competition, whereas Ellie had so many family members there to cheer her on – even if Aunt Lizzie wasn't part of them. She just had to do her very best not to let them all down.

CHAPTER
Twenty-Four

Ellie woke the next day feeling more nervous than ever. Oleg again insisted all the gymnasts have a good breakfast. Ellie attempted to munch her way dutifully through cereal and toast, but her mouth was so dry she could barely swallow. Then Sasha appeared holding parcels for both her and Katya.

'These just arrived at the hotel,' she said. 'Special delivery for Miss Trengilly and Miss Popolova!'

'Ooh – presents!' said Katya.

'Wow!' said Ellie, turning over her parcel which was identical to Katya's, both in pink packaging bearing the name of her favourite leotard brand. 'But who can they be from?'

'Open them and see!' said Bella as the others crowded round to take a peek.

Both girls tore open their parcels to reveal brand new competition leotards inside.

Katya's was gold, black and purple and was patterned to look like a ring-master's bolero jacket, studded with millions of tiny gems that sparkled the same violet colour as Katya's eyes.

'Wow! Zat is gorgeous!' said Camille. 'So chic!'

'Is perfect!' Katya sighed.

'Come on! Open yours!' said Kashvi to Ellie, leaning over excitedly.

Ellie slid off the tissue paper to reveal the most beautiful competition leotard she'd ever seen. Patterned with orange, cerise and gold swirls, set against a background of midnight black and encrusted with gems, it was brighter and bolder than anything she'd ever worn before. And she knew as soon as she looked at it that was just right for her routine. It captured the sparkle, the glamour and the danger of the moves that Casey had devised for her perfectly.

'It's . . . amazing!' she sighed.

'Is from my father!' Katya squeaked excitedly as she pulled out a note tucked inside hers. 'And everyone at circus!'

'I can't believe he sent me one too!' said Ellie, overwhelmed by the generosity of the gift.

'I expect it to say thank you for looking after me,' said Katya, matter-of-factly. 'And taking me to your home at Christmas.'

'Still, it's amazing . . .' said Ellie, unable to take her eyes off the beautiful leotard. It felt like it belonged to her already.

'Ooh, I can't decide which one I like best!' said Bella.

'They're both lovely, but there's no time to chat leos now,' said Sasha. 'We need to get you girls to the arena, or the competition will start without you!'

Ellie pulled on her new tracksuit jacket – the one Nancy and Tam had given her for Christmas – and pushed the beautiful new leotard into her kit bag. She had to wear it!

*

The atmosphere at the arena was electric. Crowds of gym fans gathered outside and there were hundreds of little girls in club tracksuits, or wearing T-shirts saying things like 'Gym Star' or 'Keep Calm and Carry on Tumbling', thronging through the doors of the arena.

Ellie could see some of them looking at her admiringly as she made her way in by the competitors' entrance. With her hair tightly pulled back in a doughnut and wearing her club tracksuit she looked like a gymnast but even after the *Gymnast* magazine piece, she wasn't a face that many people recognised. Not like Eva Reddle, the reigning British champ, who arrived just behind the Academy squad with the other Liverpool girls.

Ellie could hear little girls squeaking Eva's name excitedly as she approached.

'Can we have your autograph, Eva?'

'Go Liverpool girls!'

Lexi ran over to give her old Liverpool teammates a quick hug.

'But you're an Academy Girl now!' said Kashvi,

grinning cheekily, when she returned.

'All the way!' laughed Lexi happily.

Ellie glanced behind where Eva was signing autographs, chatting to all the little girls and being really kind. She looked up, caught Ellie watching her and smiled. Ellie smiled warmly back. After all, it must be hard turning up as the reigning champ and having to defend your title, knowing that there were sharks like Scarlett snapping at your heels, desperate to steal your crown.

During the warm-up session, Ellie looked around for Casey. She saw her off at a distance, talking to the coach from Bristol Hawks, but by time Ellie was able to go and talk to her, Casey had gone.

Then, when the warm-up came to an end, the gymnasts were sent off to change into their competition kit. The arena was already pretty full and buzzing. Ellie couldn't believe how many spectators had come early to watch the warm-up.

'And just you wait and see what happens when ze real show starts,' said Camille as they made their way to the changing rooms.

'It'll blow your mind,' Bella said. 'You feel like a rockstar.'

Ellie pulled on her new leotard and caught sight of herself in the mirror. It fitted perfectly, and in it she looked different somehow – the electric colours lit up her pale face and made her look more sophisticated. She barely recognised herself.

'Wow!' said Camille. 'Eet ees stunning!'

'And so is that!' said Bella, as Katya wiggled into her circus-style leo.

'What's the big deal?' said Scarlett, who was looking them up and down with scowl on her face. 'My parents send me new leos all the time.'

'Are they here supporting you today?' asked Kashvi.

Scarlett coloured as pink as Ellie's leotard.

'I though you said zey were coming?' asked Camille. 'What happened?'

Scarlett flushed even pinker. 'There was a last-minute change of plan,' she said quickly. 'They would have done anything to be here, but their work schedules just wouldn't allow it.'

Scarlett's eyes were bright with what looked almost like tears. For the first time ever, Ellie felt slightly sorry for her.

'Then I guess you understand why Katya's leo means so much to her,' she said, not unkindly. 'Cos her family can't be here either.'

Scarlett looked like she was about to say something in reply, but then one of the organisers appeared and the gymnasts were ushered out of the changing room and told to line up in the backstage area, ready for their big entrance.

'Showtime,' she heard Robbie say as the lights in the arena dropped and dramatic music started blaring out of the speakers all around them.

Ellie's heart was in her mouth as the gymnasts were led out on to a darkened stage at the far end of the auditorium.

'Welcome to the biggest event in the gymnastics calendar!' shouted the presenter and the crowd roared and clapped. 'This is the showdown we've all been waiting for. The battle of the best. It's the Junior British Championships!'

Again the crowd stamped and cheered and Ellie, standing in the dark beside the other girls, felt herself going weak at the knees. She hadn't expected anything like this. It was more like a rock concert than a competition.

'He is ring master in circus!' Katya whispered excitedly.

'We're up next,' whispered Bella.

'What do we do?' mumbled Ellie, terrified.

'Just copy everyone else!'

'And enjoy your moment in ze spotlight,' said Camille.

As she said this, the spotlight swung over to the stage where the girls were standing and the crowd cheered as the presenter cried, 'Let's introduce the stars of the show – here are *the gymnasts!*'

Then presenter was calling out each gymnast's name, and as the spotlight fell on each girl she stepped forwards and the crowd cheered. Suddenly Ellie's heart started beating super fast. She wished she knew where her family and Nancy were sitting in the sea of faces.

'And last year's Junior British Champ, hoping to hold on to her crown this year . . . it's Eva Reddle!' The crowd roared their approval and Ellie could see a huge banner over in one corner of the auditorium that read 'Go Eva – you're our Champ!'

Then it was the Academy girls' turn. Scarlett waved to the crowd like a pop star, Katya lapped up the applause like milk, blowing kisses and doing a little curtsey. Then Bella, Kashvi, Camille . . . they all presented and took their applause.

Ellie knew she was next in the spotlight – and she froze.

'Ellie.'

Ellie turned and saw Tam right behind her. He was in his Academy tracksuit, the familiar blue and white reassuring. 'Forget all this stuff,' he whispered. 'It's just fancy dress. It's only a competition. Right?'

Ellie looked out and saw the familiar apparatus laid out in front of her. Tam was right. It might be the biggest arena Ellie had ever been to, and the crowd might be five times the size of any she'd ever performed in front of before, but despite the lights and the noise it was just another gymnastics comp.

She heard Tam say, 'Good luck,' but when she turned he was gone and Ellie realised she hadn't wished him luck in return. But it was too late to run after him. And as the full force of the spotlight hit Ellie, she knew it was also too late to run away!

CHAPTER
Twenty-Five

Ellie was in the same rotation as Eva Reddle and her teammate Willow Hall, a gymnast called Jasmine from Bristol Hawks, and Katya, Camille and Bella. They were starting on the vault. Katya was bouncing up and down, bubbling with so much energy that Ellie thought she might explode before the competition was over. But Ellie couldn't feel excited. All she could think about was not messing up. This was her big chance and she couldn't afford to make a single mistake.

Eva Reddle was up first. Gymnasts only performed one vault for the all-around competition, but if they wanted to qualify for apparatus finals they performed a second in order to demonstrate their variety. Eva's first was a double twisting Yurchenko, and it was incredible.

'Surely she can't top that,' whispered Kashvi.

But then they watched as Eva followed it with a near-perfect Tsukahara two-and-a-half twist to earn a score of 14.85.

'How is anyone going to follow that?' asked Bella.

But somebody had to, and that was Katya. She was performing just one simple vault – she knew she stood no chance of making vault finals and all she needed to do was stay tight and land in the corridor.

Ellie watched Katya's face as she stood at the side of the run-up, waiting to be told to go. She looked fiercely determined – not the crazy little monkey who had shimmied up ropes and misbehaved in the gym when she first arrived, but a girl who wanted to win a medal here as much as any of the gymnasts who had been doing it all their lives. Vault might not be her strongest piece, but Katya was going to give it all she had.

And then Katya was off, flying towards the vault. Ellie noticed how much straighter and stronger she looked than when she had first arrived at the Academy. She hit the vault hard and ricocheted up into the air, twisting just once then landing in the corridor without a stumble.

Ellie was up next, and she was more grateful than ever for Oleg's strict training regime. She had practised her vault so often it was embedded in her muscle memory and she could do it on autopilot. Which was good, because she was so nervous she might not have been able to command her body to do anything otherwise.

She landed without a stumble, and when her score appeared it was better than she'd dared hope. Not as good as Eva's, of course, but a really strong start.

Kashvi and Bella also vaulted well and Oleg was beaming as the girls moved around to the next rotation, the crowd clapping along and waving banners that carried messages of support for their favourite gymnasts. Ellie was so overwhelmed that

229

she didn't realise for a moment that Eva Reddle was talking to her. 'So, Lexi tells me you're Lizzie Trengilly's niece, right?'

'Um – yes.'

'She's the reason I became a gymnast,' said Eva with a warm smile. 'It looks like you've inherited her talent. Your vault was beautiful. Good luck with the rest, OK?'

'Um – thanks – you too,' said Ellie.

And then they were at the bars. During warm-up Ellie reminded Katya of the things they'd worked on in the gym. 'Think like you're on the trapeze,' Ellie said.

'I do exactly like you show me,' said Katya who was looking a bit despondent. The first rotation rankings had just appeared on the big screen with her name near the bottom.

'Don't worry about that,' said Ellie. 'You've got your best pieces to come.'

Katya beamed and wrapped her arms around Ellie's waist, squeezing her tight. 'But you are seventh!' she said. 'Look!'

'There's a long way to go yet,' said Ellie. 'And a lot of great gymnasts competing for the top ten spots.'

At the top of the leaderboard was Eva Reddle, with Scarlett, who had started on beam, in second place, an Irish gymnast called Niamh in third and Camille in fourth. Kashvi and Bella were also in the top ten. It was a great start for the Academy.

Eva Reddle was up first on the bars and she was supreme once more. Then it was Katya's turn. When she mounted the bars and completed her routine without error, Ellie felt ridiculously proud of her.

'I did it!' squeaked Katya excitedly.

'You sure did!'

'And so will you!' said Katya. 'You will be so good you will make it to bars apparatus final! I just know it!'

Ellie hoped so much that she was right. She was desperate to make the apparatus finals on her favourite piece. And if she wanted to rank top five in the all-around, she was relying on a big score on bars too. There was a lot riding on the next ninety seconds.

But nothing is certain in gymnastics, and Ellie seemed to go wrong from the start. She mounted awkwardly, then was unable to find her rhythm in the giants. She was conscious of the audience watching her every move, all those eyes picking out every single mistake. Then she launched into the difficult catch-and-release move that Toni Nimakov had once so admired. But she'd misjudged slightly. She missed her hold and felt herself about to crash out. And then she was on the floor.

Ellie pulled herself to her feet, her face aflame. The fall had cost her a whole point deduction – but it had also shattered her confidence. She had to keep her focus and complete the routine, but she knew she'd blown any chance of making bar finals – and she might have blown the whole competition too.

She took a deep breath and remounted. She couldn't shake the horrible sick feeling in her stomach now and it took all her focus to keep the routine clean. When she came to the complicated dismount she was sure she was going to bottle it.

'Come on, Ellie!' shouted Katya. 'Land it tight!'

Ellie completed the dismount with only a small stumble, but she landed feeling incredibly frustrated. She'd done the same routine a thousand times in training and she knew she could execute it perfectly. Why hadn't she been able to find her rhythm today? Instead of announcing herself to the Team GB selectors as a bar-worker to pay attention to, she'd landed flat on her face.

She waited for her score to appear on the TV screen next to the judges' table. Because she had such a high difficulty score it wasn't a complete disaster, but it was nowhere near as good as it could have been if she'd nailed the execution too. By the end of the rotation she'd slipped down to tenth place in the rankings.

Ellie knew she had to put aside her disappointment and focus on the next two rotations. If she could get through them both without a single mistake, then maybe . . . maybe she might still be in with a chance.

CHAPTER
Twenty-Six

It didn't help that they had to sit out a rotation before the beam. The wait made Ellie even more nervous. Meanwhile, Katya was high as a kite after her success on the bars and she could barely contain her excitement, skipping around, trying out her floor moves, hugging Ellie and the other girls and behaving like the little monkey Ellie was used to.

Ellie tried to concentrate on stretching and deep-breathing techniques to ward off her nerves. She wished she could just block out the audience, but it was impossible not to be aware of the sea of faces on all sides of the auditorium. Then, as her eyes scanned the seating stands, she caught sight of something she hadn't noticed before. In the far corner, over by the beam, was a giant sparkly banner draped over the railings saying, 'Go, Ellie, Go!' Next to it was another saying, 'Rock it, Tam!' and third which read, 'Stick it, Katya!' Ellie's face broke into a smile as she saw Nancy and Lucy sitting behind the banners, decked out in the Academy colours of blue and silver, with little As painted on each cheek.

They caught sight of Ellie and waved madly. Ellie's heart soared. Mum and Dad were there too, and Mandy, who gave her a massive thumbs up then pointed towards the other end of the arena where Tam's name had just been announced.

Ellie turned to see Tam mounting the pommel horse. Glancing up at the board, she saw that he was in bronze medal position. The concentration on his face was intense. Ellie saw the strength it must take to maintain his momentum. She willed him to keep going.

'Wow!' she heard one of the Liverpool girls say. 'He's really good.'

'*And* really good looking,' said another girl from Cardiff GC. They both giggled.

Ellie looked away. It was so weird to hear them talking about Tam like that. Tam was . . . well, Tam. Nancy's brother, one of her best friends – or at least, he used to be.

'It is like world premiere,' Katya said to Ellie as the beam warm-up came to an end. Her face was deadly serious as she announced: 'I show world that new superstar has arrived on the beam and her name is Katya Popolova!'

Ellie smiled. If anyone else had said something like that, they would have sounded totally arrogant, but Katya spoke so matter-of-factly that it was impossible not to believe her.

'You can't wait to go out there and stun the crowd, can you?' said Ellie.

'I am going to dazzle them so they cheer me louder than anyone else in whole auditorium!' said Katya.

And dazzle them she did. Eva Reddle had

opened the rotation with an incredible beam routine that nearly toppled Scarlett off the number one spot, and the crowd went wild for it. But then Katya stepped up and put the other two firmly in the shade.

And the audience loved it. They gasped and oohed and aahed – every other performer in the arena was forgotten. And when Katya landed, everyone in the arena knew they'd just witnessed the birth of a new star. Ellie felt as if her heart might burst with happiness for her friend.

'How was that?' asked Katya, eyes alight with excitement as she ran off the podium to cheers and stamps of applause.

'It was electric!' said Ellie. 'Just take a look over there at Scarlett. She looks as if she's ready to kill you, which proves just how awesome you were!'

Sure enough when Katya's beam score appeared on the screen, Scarlett, who was over by the vault, flushed bright pink as she realised Katya – a year her junior – had just gone into first place on the beam.

Ellie's beam went even worse than her bar. She

misjudged a simple split leap and tumbled off the beam before she'd even started her acro section. Then she under-rotated in her double-back and fell off again. As she remounted for the third time she felt as if all her dreams were slipping away from her and there was nothing she could do to stop them. She finished the routine without further stumbles, but the two falls had cost her dearly and she was now down in twelfth place.

So there was just the floor left and it was her last chance – she couldn't afford to mess up again.

As they made their way round for the final rotation, she passed the boys and Tam gave her a grin. 'Nice leotard,' he said. 'Now go and make her proud on the floor!'

'What?' said Ellie, turning quickly, confused by his strange comment. 'Who . . .? Who do I need to make proud?'

But they had passed in a flash and there was no time to find out what Tam had been going on about. He was already moving on to the vault and Ellie found herself standing in front of the floor, staring at the blue space – knowing everything rested on what she could do there.

Katya's floor routine caused almost as big a sensation as her beam. Sasha's choreography, matched with Katya's incredible tumbling skills, made for a dazzling combination. Crazy, eclectic, funny and full of variety, it was amazing to watch as she wiggled, clicked and span through Russian Cossack moves before emerging into a cheeky cha-cha, complete with jazz hands. The routine was as crazy and brilliant as Katya herself, but it also had moments of real pathos, fire and love, and at those moments Ellie realised that Sasha really did understand Katya better than anyone else at the Academy.

It seemed as if the crowd would never stop clapping and Katya lapped it all up, waving and doing a little curtsey. And when she ran off the podium she flew into Sasha's arms and covered her with kisses. 'That was best thing ever!' she giggled. 'Better even than circus – better than horses and trapeze and clown – best feeling in whole world!'

'I'm glad you enjoyed it!' laughed Sasha. 'Let's hope the judges did too!'

'How could they not like that?' said Bella. 'She brought the house down!'

'There was still quite a bit of precision lacking in some of those tumbles, cupcake,' smiled Sasha. 'Although you did a very good job of disguising that with all your razzmatazz!'

Katya smiled and hugged her harder than ever. Ellie remembered how Katya had declared that she would never like her coach – now all that had changed!

The scores came in and Katya had taken ninth place on the floor. She'd secured two spots in the apparatus finals. Considering she'd only started at the Academy last term, it was an amazing achievement.

And Ellie was up next.

Suddenly she couldn't help wishing Nancy were down there next to her, instead of up in the stands. She would have made some funny joke that would have sent Ellie to the floor with laughter in her heart. But she wasn't. Today, in the middle of the giant crowd, Ellie was on her own.

She stepped up on to the floor and took her position in the middle of the stage. The routine started with her body curled, hands wrapped around her head. As she lay there, her heart hammering, she couldn't seem to think about sparkle or artistry or performance – all she could think was that she mustn't mess up again. She had to be flawless, aim for the perfect ten, not give away a single deduction.

As the music began, her limbs slowly unfolded, 'like a flower opening,' as Casey described it. Then, as the music shifted between violins and a sound like raindrops, Ellie span into the corner for her first tumble sequence. That was when the music broke into a faster, funkier rhythm and Ellie's movements were no longer fluid and balletic but angular and punchy.

The thing about performing on the floor was that all eyes were on you. Ellie knew that Mum, Dad and Lucy were seeing her new routine for the first time, and she knew they were all willing her to do well. But Barbara Steele was watching too – and the other national squad selectors. And Ellie only had this one last piece of apparatus to make an impression on, to announce herself to the crowd as a new star of the gymnastics universe. Only Ellie still wasn't sure she felt like a star.

All the same, she was determined to go for it – to throw everything she had into this final performance. She moved with a kind of desperate energy, putting all her anxieties, her hopes, her fears into her movements. But even when she nailed the complicated tumble at the start and heard the crowd cheer their approval, she couldn't relax. She executed her leap series and her turns perfectly and then went into a two-and-a-half twisting tumble sequence which earned her maximum points. She knew it was good, and the crowd liked it, cheering loudly as she landed – but she was too frightened of making a mistake to enjoy it.

Ellie could hear a voice in her head telling her to smile, to acknowledge the crowd, to open herself up to them, but all she could think of was getting everything right. She knew her face was a blank mask, that she wasn't even smiling, that her eyes were downcast, shutting the audience out, not letting them in.

She landed her final tumble sequence without a stumble and span into the final turn before flinging herself on the floor for the finale. She could hear the audience clapping. She knew she'd done well, she hadn't made a single error – so why did she just feel like crying?

Then the scores were out and she was amazed to see she was in fourth place on the floor, earning a place in the apparatus finals. It was amazing, but it wasn't enough to get her into the overall top ten. Her heart sank. She knew that she had no right to be disappointed – she'd messed up on bar and fallen off the beam (twice!) – but still, it was hard not to feel heartbroken.

The Academy girls huddled together, watching the big screen as the last few remaining scores came in and the final rankings were calculated. Eva

Reddle took first place, with Scarlett in second, Camille in third, Willow Hall in fourth and Bella and Kashvi in joint fifth. Camille was jumping for joy, hugging Kashvi and Bella and babbling away incomprehensibly in French. Scarlett just glared and when Eva came over to shake her hand and congratulate her, Scarlett tipped her head to one side and said simply, 'I suppose you got lucky today.' Then she turned sharply away and marched off with her nose in the air.

'Don't mind her,' Ellie found herself saying to Eva. 'She's like that with everyone. You totally deserved to win.'

'You were great too,' said Eva.

'Thanks,' said Ellie quietly. She couldn't help feeling Eva was just being polite.

She was genuinely pleased for the others, though, and even more excited when the boys' overall rankings appeared and she saw that Tam had taken silver, only missing out on the top spot by the smallest of margins. She wanted to go over and congratulate him, but he was being lifted up in the air by all the boys' squad and didn't even glance in her direction.

Ellie looked around at the arena and wondered if people would be disappointed in her. Emma, Sasha, Oleg – she'd let them all down. She'd never been quite good enough all along. And now she'd proved it once and for all.

CHAPTER
Twenty-Seven

Whilst the other girls ran off to get ready for the presentation of the awards, Ellie slowly gathered her stuff and made her way backstage towards the changing rooms. She'd been so looking forward to seeing Nancy and her family again, but now even that felt spoilt somehow. Not looking where she was going, Ellie bumped straight into someone. It was Casey Cottrell.

'Hey, Ellie! Well done out there. You really nailed those tumbles.'

'Oh – um – thanks,' said Ellie, unable to meet her eye.

'You looked a bit nervous, but that's only to be expected,' Casey was saying. 'This is your first time at a big event like this, right?

Ellie nodded.

Casey was smiling. 'The spotlight takes a bit of getting used to, doesn't it?'

Ellie wanted to try and explain that she just didn't feel comfortable with the routine, no matter how hard she tried, but for some reason her voice didn't seem to be working.

'I see you got the parcel OK?' said Casey.

'What?' Ellie looked up in confusion.

'The leotard Lizzie chose for you – to wish you luck.'

'I – but . . .' Ellie stammered. 'I . . . I thought it was from Katya's father!'

'No – definitely from Lizzie,' Casey smiled. 'I helped her pick it out so it would match your routine. Didn't you get her note?'

'What note?' Ellie hadn't remembered there being any kind of letter. Just the parcel – identical to Katya's in every way, or that's what she'd thought.

'She was sorry she couldn't make it here herself,' Casey was saying. 'She'll be watching you on gymnastics TV though, cheering you on from California.'

Ellie could barely take in what Casey was saying. Lizzie did care after all. She knew all about Ellie's routine, and she was watching from thousands of miles away.

'Lizzie's doing a bit of coaching over there. One of the university teams,' Casey explained. 'She's got the makings of a first-class coach. She's even been talking to Emma about coming to the Academy.'

There were tears pooling in Ellie's eyes, threatening to fall. 'I – I still don't get it.'

'She explained everything in her letter,' said Casey. 'Look, I have to dash for the medal ceremony, but that routine of yours – it's so nearly there, you know.'

'Is it?' asked Ellie, barely able to believe that what she was saying could be true.

'It got you to the floor finals, didn't it?'

'Yes – um – that is – I suppose.'

'You know, it's OK to make mistakes – all gymnasts do. Even Lizzie!'

'Really?' Ellie could barely imagine the great Lizzie Trengilly messing up like she had today. Even her fall in the Olympic finals had been because of injury, not a mistake.

'Of course. Every gymnast has a bad competition sometimes,' said Casey with a smile. 'The sign of a good gymnast is the ability to keep going, even when things are going wrong.'

Ellie nodded.

'And a *great* gymnast doesn't always have to be perfect,' Casey went on. 'She brings a star quality to her work that lights up the whole arena and blots out any tiny errors.'

'But what if I don't have star quality?' said Ellie quietly.

Casey smiled. 'When you perform, you are telling stories in your head,' she said. 'Am I right?'

Ellie nodded. 'Yes – I mean . . . not today, but sometimes.'

'Lizzie always did the same.' Casey smiled again.

'But she also knew how to share the story with the audience. You need to do the same. Forget about precision and perfect tens. You have practiced so hard you can do that in your sleep. Let all that go, immerse yourself in the magic, and don't forget to let the audience in too. That's what true stars do. They sprinkle a bit of their stardust over everyone who watches them. And you have the makings of a star, Ellie Trengilly, which means you have plenty of stardust to share.'

'Really?' Ellie stammered.

'Really! Don't be afraid of the spotlight,' said Casey. 'It's your time to take centre stage!'

And with that she was gone, leaving Ellie's head spinning.

Suddenly Katya came hurtling through the door and squealed. 'There you are! Everyone is waiting for you! They think you is getting lost – come on!'

And Ellie found herself being dragged out to the foyer where Mum, Dad, Lucy, Nancy and Mandy were all waiting for her, their faces wreathed in smiles. Lucy flew to give her a cuddle and then everyone was congratulating her on how well she'd done, saying how proud they were. Ellie was thrilled to see everyone but despite what Casey had just said to her she still felt a bit like a fraud. She wasn't a superstar, she was just Ellie.

When Nancy pulled her into a giant hug, Ellie noticed her friend was taller than ever. 'Nancy, you've grown since Christmas!'

'I know. It's the Cornish air – and your mum's pasties!' said Nancy with a giant grin. Her face had a ruddy glow to it and she looked happier and more relaxed than ever.

'Don't talk to me about food,' said Tam, who had emerged from the boys' changing room with a silver medal strung around his neck. He was looking tired but happy. 'I'm absolutely starving! Gymnastics is hungry work, you know.'

'Don't worry – I brought some pasties for you!' said Ellie's mum.

'And I've got some of Mario's flapjack,' said Mandy. 'He sent it specially. And chocolate fudge cake for Katya too!'

251

Katya gave a squeak of happiness and Tam punched the air happily. 'Pasties, cake and flapjack!' He grinned. 'What more can I ask for? You know, I don't even think I care that Nancy is taller than me now.'

'Me neither!' said Nancy. 'I don't need to worry about getting too tall any more.'

'In fact, the taller the better if she's going to be an Olympic rower,' Dad agreed with a smile.

Ellie beamed and wrapped her arms around her friend. 'It is *so* good to see you again, Nance!' she said. 'We've all missed you like mad.'

'Well, I wouldn't say *all*,' said Tam.

'Come on, *little* bro!' said Nancy, pulling herself up to her full height so that she towered over her twin. 'You must have missed me a teeny weeny bit?'

'Nope!' said Tam with a shrug. 'You know how they say that when twins are separated they feel like they've lost an arm or a leg or something?'

'Is that how you feel?' asked Lucy who had been busily catching up with Katya and now had her arms around the radiant-looking circus girl.

'No, I just got rid of a giant pain in the bottom!'
Tam replied.

Lucy and Katya giggled while Nancy punched her
brother on the arm. But the two were both grinning
and clearly delighted to see each other, even though
neither of them was going to admit it.

'So – um – what do we do now?' asked Ellie. The
next day was a rest day whilst the Seniors competed,
and then it was apparatus finals on Sunday.

'Well, after we've had something to eat – lots
to eat – me and Katya have a surprise for you all,'
said Tam.

'Yes!' Katya beamed at Tam. 'Is big treat!'

'What? What?' demanded Lucy, alight with
curiosity.

'Uh-oh – I'm not sure I'm going to like the sound
of this!' said Nancy.

'Don't worry, sis. It involves boats!'

'Um – I thought Katya hated boats?' said Lucy,
looking at Katya in astonishment.

'Yes, didn't she say she was never setting her foot
in a boat ever again?' said Ellie, who was equally

surprised and curious.

'I know. I also am very shocked,' said Katya. 'But is only way to get there.'

'Only way to get where?' asked Nancy.

'To the circus, of course!' said Tam.

'What?' Ellie glanced at Mum and Dad and Mandy. They were all smiling. They seemed to know all about Tam and Katya's circus surprise.

'Oh, stop asking questions!' said Tam. 'Let's get some food in my belly quickly or I might just have to eat one of you!'

'And you don't want to miss curtain up,' said Dad. 'Or whatever they call it in the circus!'

CHAPTER
Twenty-Eight

Less than an hour later, after they'd wolfed down pizzas and talked through every single second of the day's competition, the twins, Ellie, Lucy and Katya were waving goodbye to their parents and climbing on board the ferry that would take them to the other side of the River Mersey. Katya looked seasick from the moment she stepped on board, but she did not mutter a word of complaint.

'So, when exactly did you come up with this plan?' Ellie asked Tam. He was being completely normal again now that Nancy was back.

'Remember when we were doing the clown

school,' said Tam, 'and Harry told us that he was going off to perform in a show?'

Ellie nodded.

'Well, we were chatting afterwards and he said it was near Liverpool, so I figured we had to come and see it.'

'And circus owner is old friend of my father,' Katya added. 'So he give us tickets. Like I tell you, circus is one big family!'

'So you two planned this together?' said Ellie, looking from one to the other.

'We want it to be big surprise for everyone!' said Katya. 'Especially you, Ellie. Because you help me so much and I want to say thank you!'

Ellie smiled and caught Tam's eye. He just shrugged and grinned.

They went up and sat on the deck of the boat, looking out at the vast expanse of the River Mersey and the gleaming docks on either side.

'It's like the creek – only a hundred times bigger!' said Nancy.

'Yeah – that giant ship yard is like Dad's

boatshed . . .' said Lucy.

'And the docks are like a bigger version of the quay at the sailing club . . .' added Tam.

'Only I wouldn't like to do a gym routine on them like you did at the regatta,' said Lucy. 'Just think how far you'd fall if you took a tumble!'

'Well, I'm not planning on doing any gym routines anywhere,' said Nancy cheerfully. 'It's all boats, boats, boats for me nowadays – not a single roly-poly or somersault in sight!'

'Which reminds me, I loved your new routine, Ellie!' said Lucy.

'Did you?' asked Ellie, looking out across the river towards the sea in the distance. 'Casey reckons I still need a bit more sparkle.'

'Well, there's plenty of sparkle at the circus,' said Tam. 'Let's see if we can pick you some up tonight!'

Ellie and Lucy had never actually been to a real circus before, and even the time she'd spent at Circus Pocus hadn't prepared Ellie for the magic of

257

the live show. Katya had got them ringside seats so they were right up close to the action, and as the lights dropped and the drumroll announced the entrance of the ringmaster, Ellie was reminded of the dramatic opening to Junior British Championships. For a second she experienced a moment of fear at the thought of stepping back into the spotlight at the apparatus finals.

But all her fears were quickly forgotten as she fell under the magic spell of the show. The clowns entranced, the acrobats amazed, the strongmen made her eyes boggle and the magician left them all mystified. It was a feast for all the senses: colourful, musical, exotic, exciting, magical and incredible!

And as Ellie watched the gorgeous glittering aerial artistes spin on silks and fling themselves from trapeze to trapeze like exotic plumed birds, she realised she wasn't watching their technique. She wasn't thinking about whether their legs were straight or their bums tucked under. She just fell under their spell. They were telling a story and the crowd was allowed to be part of that tale they wove, part of their magic. It was just as Casey had said.

And just when Ellie felt as if she might burst with the wonder of it all, something even madder happened.

Ellie recognised Harry as soon as the clown leapt on to the stage. Even in full make-up, with his clown suit on, she'd have known him anywhere by his familiar accent.

And when he came to his grand finale, Ellie heard him announce that he needed some helpers. 'But luckily I gotta coupla young'uns in the audience today who I've been trainin' up to be mighty fine clown helpers!' he declared.

The audience clapped and Ellie turned to Tam. 'Does he – mean us?'

'I've got an awful feeling he does!' said Tam.

Suddenly Ellie found the spotlight glaring in her eyes for the second time that day. Her stomach did a backflip.

'So, come on down to the stage, Harry's little helpers!' Harry was saying. Katya didn't need asking twice. She was in the ring, bouncing round with excitement, within seconds. Ellie just wanted to curl up and disappear.

'I need all three of you!' said Harry, grinning at them with his giant clown smile. 'Come on, folks. Give 'em a big hand to get them out in the ring!'

The audience started clapping and cheering, and Ellie had a feeling there was no getting out of this.

'Go on!' said Nancy.

'I don't think we've got any choice in the matter,' said Tam, as the audience started to stamp their feet and cheer louder than ever. Tam grabbed Ellie's hand and tugged her into the ring, and the audience roared their approval as Harry shook hands solemnly with each of them in turn.

The act was the one they'd practised in circus school – Harry on his giant unicycle balancing plates which they had to throw up to him whilst turning somersaults in a circle around the ring.

'Are you up for it?' shouted Harry who had mounted his bike and was wobbling to and fro, veering crazily from side to side and looking for all the world as if he was about to fall off and land in the audience's lap at any moment. But Ellie knew he wouldn't.

'Are we up for it?' said Tam, looking at the others.

Katya nodded. Performing in the ring came as naturally to her as breathing. Ellie looked around her. The cheers of the crowd, the magic web spun by the other performers in the ring – it all made her feel giddy and reckless. She nodded too.

'Let's go then!' said Tam. He picked up a plate and showed it to the audience, pulling a funny face and shrugging as if he had no idea what he was doing. The audience laughed, then cheered as Tam tucked it between his teeth and took off, crossing the ring in a tumble sequence before tossing the first plate up to Harry. He caught it deftly, to gasps of disbelief from the audience. They definitely hadn't expected that!

Then Katya was off, flipping over and over before delivering a plate to Harry and taking her applause with a little shimmy and a backflip.

And then it was Ellie's turn. She could feel the audience looking at her and suddenly she knew what she had to do. She had to pretend she was a circus performer – like one of the exotically plumed aerial artistes who had spun and dazzled – to forget she just a girl wearing an old tracksuit. She had to dream she was a circus girl and invite the audience into the dream with her. And if she dropped a plate – well, the big top wasn't going to collapse on her head, was it!

She threw a teacup in the air and caught it in her teeth with a flourish. Then she was off, tumbling once, twice, three times, then sending the cup spinning upwards, feeding off the thunder of applause as Harry pretended to drink a cup of tea.

After that, it was easy. One after another they spun, tumbled, somersaulted and sent crockery flying as Harry's pile of spinning plates rose higher and higher. They finished with a daring triple sequence which they'd only practiced a couple of times at Circus Pocus – and messed up each and every time!

'Do you reckon we can do it tonight?' asked Tam.

Ellie could see her own glowing face reflected

in Katya's shining eyes. She felt as if anything was possible.

'We might as well go for it!' she said.

And the audience seemed to think so too, cheering and clapping as the three assistants each took a plate and held them up in the air. And then they were off, spinning up, round, over and then sending three plates up into the air all at the same time.

It was messy and the timing was off but somehow Harry managed to catch the plates – one, two, three! The audience went mad, and then suddenly there were plates raining down over their heads as Harry sent the whole pile deliberately flying in a shower over the ring. The audience laughed and cheered and Ellie felt their energy pouring into her, lifting her. Tam was laughing and Katya hugged her hard before the three of them took a bow. Ellie didn't think she'd ever felt more alive in her whole life.

'You were all amazing!' said Lucy as they emerged later from the big top, still buzzing with the energy of the circus.

'Although I think Tam would look better in one of those big feathery headdresses the trapeze girls wore!' said Nancy.

'Or maybe a spangly leotard!' giggled Lucy. 'Covered in jewels!'

'With feathers on his bottom,' added Katya and the girls all fell about laughing.

They made their way back across the blackened waters of the river under the moonlight. Sitting on the deck of the ferry, Ellie gazed up at the stars and thought she saw them differently tonight. They looked like the dazzling sequins on her black and gold leotard, like tiny showgirls dazzling in the night.

'Do you reckon you've found your sparkle then?' asked Tam, coming to sit down beside her.

Ellie nodded. 'Now I just need to put a bit of it into my routine at floor finals.'

'And then you'll be unbeatable,' said Nancy, squeezing herself down on the other side and giving her a hug. 'Trust me!'

CHAPTER
Twenty-Nine

The next day they all went to watch the senior gymnasts compete. Sian Edwards was defending her title as Senior British Champion and Matt Simmons was out to regain the number one spot which he'd held two years ago, but had missed out on the previous year due to injury. It was impossible not to be inspired watching the older gymnasts performing moves that made Ellie's heart soar.

'Hey, Tam!' a voice sailed over from the stand above. 'Can't keep away from the love of your life, I see!'

Ellie looked up to see Robbie coming down the

aisle. Next to her she felt Tam stiffen.

'Just hanging out with my sister, Rob,' he said.

'Yeah, right!' said Robbie with a smirk in Ellie's direction. 'Any excuse to flirt with your girlfriend!'

Ellie found herself flushing and Tam looked more uncomfortable than ever, but Nancy came to the rescue. 'Robbie Sipson, I know you are the biggest gossip in the Academy, but are you seriously trying to tell me Ellie and Tam are an item?' she asked, staring at Robbie like he was an idiot.

'I dunno, you tell me,' said Robbie with a wink at Ellie.

'Well, I can tell you one thing,' said Nancy. 'No girl I know would be stupid enough to fall for my ugly mug of a brother.'

Robbie laughed.

'In fact, there's only one thing less likely than that,' Nancy went on.

'Yeah?' said Robbie, the stupid grin still plastered over his face. 'And what's that?'

'Some girl falling for you! Now go find someone else to annoy.'

'Fine,' said Robbie trying to act like it was no big deal. 'Whatever!'

'What was he even talking about?' asked Lucy, who was looking confused.

'Yeah, where on earth did he get the idea you two were – what? A thing?' said Nancy, looking from Tam to Ellie. 'I mean – yuk!'

Tam sighed and shook his head. 'OK, it started with Katya and the whole kissing issue,' he explained.

'So is my fault this boy is being mean to you?' said Katya, looking angrily after Robbie, as if she wanted to go and punch him in the nose for upsetting her hero.

'No – well, not exactly,' said Tam. 'I mean, that's when he came up with this whole joke about how I must be secretly dating one of you. We all spent so much time together.'

'Which is crazy because you're totally the ugliest boy in the universe,' said Nancy, rolling her eyes. 'But, right – go on . . .'

'It was OK until Nancy left the Academy,' Tam explained.

'Oh, I get it!' said Nancy. 'Cos then if you hung out with Ellie or Katya he'd say you must be seeing one of them?'

'Pretty much,' nodded Tam. 'Not so much Katya cos she stopped kissing me after Christmas Eve,' Tam glanced quickly at Ellie and shrugged. 'That just left Ellie . . .'

'So that's why you went off-radar?' said Ellie. 'Started avoiding me.'

'I'm sorry,' said Tam. 'It was just easier to hang out with the boys than deal with the hassle. It was rubbish of me.'

'Yeah, it was!' Nancy huffed.

Tam ignored his sister. 'Can we be mates again, Ellie?'

'Mates!' said Ellie with a smile.

'And I don't care who knows it!' said Tam, flinging an arm around Ellie and pulling her into a hug.

'I have hug too?' asked Katya hopefully.

'NO!' said all the others at once.

*

The day of apparatus finals dawned bright and clear, but with a biting cold in the air that seemed way too cold for spring.

'It feels almost cold enough for snow!' said Nancy as they made their way over to the arena. Nancy and Lucy had stayed the night with Katya and Ellie, bunking down on sleeping bags on the floor 'Hey, do you remember our snowy Christmas adventure?'

'Do not remind me,' said Katya, shuddering violently at the memory. She was quieter than normal that morning. Emma had talked to her and Ellie at breakfast and told them that Barbara Steele would be watching today's competition closely.

'It's a long shot,' added Ellie. 'But Emma says Barbara occasionally takes a reserve in the squad if she sees potential at apparatus finals.'

'What did I tell you!' Nancy said. 'And now you know you know you've got Lizzie Trengilly behind you, you'll ace it!'

Ellie smiled. She'd finally found Lizzie's note inside the parcel that the leotard had come in. It was just a coincidence that it had arrived at the same time as Katya's – the letter had been there all the time if only she'd looked for it. Reading Lizzie's note had made Ellie cry, but in a good way, because Lizzie seemed to know every detail about Ellie's gym career.

I am so proud of the gymnast you are becoming, Lizzie had written. *And I hope one day that we can work together, you and I.*

Ellie's heart had soared when she read that. She couldn't think of anything she'd like more. But then Lizzie had gone on. *I have kept my distance because you deserve to be a star in your own right, and I know you have more than enough talent and determination to make it on your own – even if you don't realise it yet.* Ellie sighed. How she longed to believe that Lizzie was right. *But I've always been watching, cheering you on from the sidelines. Never forget that.*

As Ellie stood on the stage in the arena that morning, waiting for her name to be announced, she remembered Lizzie's words and reminded herself that the audience had come here today to see a spectacle. To be amazed, dazzled, just like the audience at the circus. There were little girls in the crowd who were just learning to do cartwheels and round-offs. They weren't calculating deductions, looking for tiny errors – they just wanted to sit and gaze at the incredible routines and dream of performing here too one day. Ellie's job was to weave a magical story on stage and to share it with all those little daydreamers in the audience, to allow them to be part of the enchantment she wove on the blue floor.

The apparatus finals went in the usual Olympic order – vault, bar, beam and finally floor – so Ellie had to wait for the final rotation before she got to perform. It was tough watching the finalists go out for the bar final, knowing that she could be have been one of them, knowing too that her routine might just have been good enough to win her a medal, or to gain the attention of the GB selectors. But it was no use thinking about that today. Thanks to Casey, she still had a chance to make an impression on floor.

So when Kashvi came away with gold on the bars,

Ellie was genuinely thrilled for her. And when Katya stepped out for the beam rotation, Ellie wished her good luck and meant it with all her heart.

Apparatus finals results rarely work out quite the same as the all-around competition. A gymnast can come top on a piece of apparatus in the all-around, then perform the same routine at apparatus finals and not get the top spot.

'It is all about one single performance on the day,' Oleg reminded the girls as they got ready to perform. 'Nothing else before or afterwards counts. Is no good saying, "But I did it way better in practice yesterday". Judges not care about that!'

And he was right. Eva Reddle messed up her beam completely. And when Katya performed, although she was still dazzling there, were a few little wobbles that cost her points. She only came third in the end, whilst Scarlett claimed the top spot, with Niamh the Irish gymnast taking second.

But Katya was as thrilled as if she'd won Olympic gold, squeaking and bouncing for joy. 'I win medal, Ellie! I win medal!'

'I'm so pleased for you!' said Ellie. 'And now you can go out and get another one on the floor!'

'Oh no!' said Katya, her face serious suddenly. '*You* will win gold on floor. I feel it in my magic bones.'

'Magic bones?' Ellie laughed.

'Oh yes,' Katya nodded, her face deadly serious. 'Circus girls always have magic bones and mine are telling me that today Ellie will be champion.'

'I don't know about magic bones,' said Ellie. 'But if I manage to capture a bit of circus magic today, it's all thanks to you!'

'Well, you help me conquer bars,' said Katya. 'So we are odd!'

'Do you mean even?' laughed Ellie.

'Actually, I think you're both a bit odd as well!' said Tam coming over to join them. 'But then all the best gymnasts are a bit weird. I reckon you have to be to do what we do – it's pretty mad!'

'And the best thing in the world!' added Ellie.

CHAPTER
Thirty

Ellie was last up on the floor. Watching the other girls perform their routines, she knew it would be a tall order to contend for a medal spot. But Ellie was wearing the leotard Lizzie had given her, and she wasn't going to perform frightened any more. This was her time to shine.

So she stepped on the floor and let go of everything: her worries about getting everything right, perfect tens, playing it safe, sticking to the rules, the nagging fear inside that she might not be good enough. She lay down, arms wrapped over her head, then closed her eyes and allowed herself to imagine she was in the middle of the circus ring, dressed in a jewel-encrusted outfit, with feathery wing-like arms and ostrich plume feathers on her head. She imagined there was sawdust at her feet and nothing but the canvas of the big top between her and the starry night.

As the music started and she began to unfurl, Ellie cast her eyes around the arena and invited the audience into her dream world, telling them her story. She beckoned them into the big top, invited them to share the fantasy. She forgot all about precision and technique, she could do all that on autopilot, allowing her imagination to take over. Ellie tiptoed like a fairy through the raindrops sequence, swayed like a reed through the violins and then when the music struck up tempo she flung herself into showgirl mode, announcing herself to the assembled crowd like she was a glittering superstar. The tumbles seemed to come so easily that day because she felt like an enchantress, winged and airborne, a circus girl, a gypsy, a shy duckling turned into a beautiful swan.

And for that minute and a half she forgot she was even in a competition, forgot about Barbara Steele and Team GB and the medals table and anything – everything – except her circus dream.

She delivered the routine like she had never done in her life and when the music ended she felt like crying, although she wasn't sure if it was from joy or sadness. Sadness that the dream was over, but joy because for that short time it had been hers. Being under the spotlight hadn't been terrifying as she'd always feared – it had been wonderful!

'You were incredible,' said Eva Reddle when Ellie descended from the podium, breathless and still reeling from the torrents of applause that had followed her routine. 'Breathtaking!'

'Thank you!' said Ellie.

'I came here when I was a kid and I saw your aunt perform,' said Eva. 'You reminded me of her.'

'Yes, you were beautiful – brilliant – golden!' said Katya.

And then Ellie's scores appeared on the screen. She could barely take it what they said. She could only hear Katya yelling, 'My bones are right! You win gold, Ellie! You win gold!'

And a number spinning round in her head: 14.65.

Just a tenth higher than Eva, but still enough to get her the top spot.

She'd done it. She, Ellie Trengilly, had won a gold medal. On the floor. At British Championships.

She'd dreamed of a day like this – and now somehow – incredibly, magically – her dream had come true!

The twins, plus Katya, Ellie and Lucy, sat by the old docks, staring out over the River Mersey, their legs dangling over the edge as they gazed out over the water.

'Are you excited about going home to Moscow for the holidays, Katya?' Nancy asked.

'I am hardly able to wait,' said Katya, who had a bronze medal slung around her neck. She hadn't taken it off since she'd won and had vowed to sleep in it – possibly forever. 'But I promise Sasha I not fall into old ways. I keep my back straight and practise gymnastic-walking every single day.'

'We'll miss you!' said Lucy. 'I wish we were all going to Russia – I'd love to meet your family.'

'See if they are all as bonkers as you!' laughed Tam.

Katya grinned. 'Maybe European Championships will be in Moscow, and you can come to Popolov Circus!'

Tam shrugged modestly. He had a gold medal tucked in his pocket, having beaten all the Senior gymnasts on the pommel horse at Masters. 'There's no guarantee I'll compete,' he said.

'You just beat all the seniors to win gold on pommel,' Ellie reminded him. 'There's no way they won't take you to Euros.'

'Well, you've got a place on the Junior National squad too,' Tam said with a smile. 'Unless you've forgotten already.'

Ellie's heart did a somersault. Of course she hadn't forgotten, although she could still hardly get over what had happened. Barbara Steele taking her aside after the medal ceremony and saying she'd like

Ellie to train with the Junior National Squad – as a reserve at first – but with a chance of making it into the full squad if she worked hard enough.

'Yes, but they only take five gymnasts to Euros,' said Ellie. 'And I doubt I'll be first on the list.'

'Not with that attitude you won't!' said Nancy, imitating what Emma had said to her all those months ago, before the Challenge Cup. It seemed like a lifetime ago.

Ellie couldn't help laughing because Nancy sounded so uncannily like Emma.

'Don't let me down, Ellie,' Nancy went on, switching back into Nancy mode. 'I've got a grand master plan which involves you and Tam at the Olympics in leotards and me in a rowing boat!'

'Can I come too?' asked Lucy.

'And me!' Katya piped up.

'Hmm – you might be too young for the *next* Olympics,' said Nancy. 'Mind you, I'll only be fifteen, which is too young for a rower. So I guess we'd all better aim for the one after. What do you reckon, folks?'

'Sounds like a good plan, sis,' said Tam.

'So it's all pretty simple really,' said Nancy, staring out across the river where the ferry was making its way across the glittering waves. 'We need to get Lucy into the Academy. Katya needs to make National Squad, and Ellie's got to get a spot at Europeans . . .'

'Ooh, and we is needing your Aunt Lizzie to come and coach at Academy too!' Katya added.

Ellie grinned at the mention of Lizzie's name. 'Wouldn't that be cool! I mean, I've come to kind of enjoy Sergeant Oleg's training camp but working with Lizzie . . . that would just be the best.'

Ellie looked around at her friends and smiled. At that moment she felt as if she might burst with happiness. She had a gold medal tucked safely in her pocket, a reserve place in the National Squad, and sponsorship too – enough to pay for Lucy to come to the Academy one day. Her wish had come true. And it might be a long shot but there was a chance – just a chance – that she might get to compete for her country at the Junior European Championships in the summer.

A year ago this would have seemed like an impossible dream and yet here she was, with so many new opportunities about to open up for her it was hard to believe it was all real.

But it was. And at that moment, as she gazed out over the river where the setting sun cast a glittering pink glow over the rippling waves, Ellie felt like she was standing in the wings at the circus, staring out over an empty stage, waiting for the show to begin. And she realised that she wasn't frightened of taking centre stage. Not any longer.

This was her moment. The lights were about to go up, and Ellie was ready to step into the spotlight!

Acknowledgements

With thanks to all the gymnasts, coaches and gym families at Baskervilles Gymnastics Club, particularly the lovely League Squad girlies, not forgetting the squad brothers – Archie, Will and Joe! Sasha Tilley for gymnastics/circus advice – and magnificent eyelashes! All the Challenge Cup 2013 helpers and coaches, particularly the Bury 'Stick It!' crowd and the inspirational Rebecca Moore (definitely one to watch!)

Claudia Fragapane for loveliness and words of wisdom at West Country League (and for the electric floor routines!) Lisa Mason – coolest gym mum EVER – for rocking the come-back-queen look and showing that when it comes to gymnastics, age is just a number! Nick Ruddock and the Junior GB team who let me come to national squad camp and patiently answered all my questions. Neil Burton at British Gymnastics for always keeping my gym facts straight! Everyone at BG who has been so supportive of the series, particularly the lovely Simon Evans. Neil Fox and everyone at Milano for their endless generosity and kindness.

Caroline Montgomery, Lindsey Heaven and Ali Dougal for making me a far better writer than I ever would be without them. And Jonny, Joe and Elsie – cos I love you!

Cartwheel into . . .

★ GOING FOR ★
GOLD
The exciting third book in the
Somersaults and *Dreams*
series.